Balzac's Horse

and

Other Stories

Also by Gert Hofmann

THE SPECTACLE AT THE TOWER

OUR CONQUEST

THE PARABLE OF THE BLIND

Balzac's Horse

and

Other Stories

by

GERT HOFMANN

Selected and Translated by

CHRISTOPHER MIDDLETON

Fromm International Publishing Corporation
New York

"A Conversation About Balzac's Horse"
and "Casanova and the Extra"
originally published
in *Gespräch über Balzacs Pferd*
Copyright © 1981 Residenz Verlag, Salzburg and Vienna

"Tolstoy's Head," "Moth," "The Cramp," "The Night,"
and "Arno" from manuscripts by Gert Hofmann
Copyright © 1986 Gert Hofmann, Erding/München

Designed by Jacques Chazaud

Printed in the United States of America

First U. S. Edition

Library of Congress Cataloging-in-Publication Data

Hofmann, Gert.
Balzac's horse and other stories / by Gert Hofmann; selected
and translated by Christopher Middleton.—1st U.S. ed.
p. cm.
ISBN 0-88064-074-X
1. Hofmann, Gert—Translations, English. I. Middleton,
Christopher. II. Title.
PT2668.0376A25 1988
833'.914—dc19   87-28923
                                                              CIP

Contents

Balzac's Horse

and

Other Stories

Moth

That Sunday when our butcher, Herr Netzer, has to take his daughter to the asylum—she'd tried to set fire to his shop—we all get up early and put cushions across the window ledge and lean far out. People are watching from other windows too, other people on Mutschmannstrasse. They call out to us that all night his kitchen light has been on. Now lights are being switched on in the rooms that look out on the street. One of us thinks he can see a face. Hers or his? we ask. Hers, he says, she's crying. Well, she hasn't got much time left for crying, at ten she's due at the asylum, we say and look at the clock. And we're impatient. We've taken over Czechoslovakia, now we want Danzig too. Then someone walks through all the rooms switching off the lights, one after another. We go into the kitchen and make coffee, then we look across again, but we don't see much.

All the better for hearing: Our room is perfect for hearing from. In the summertime, when Netzer's windows are open, we can hear every word. The wind carries to us not only his voice, quiet and deep, a real butcher's voice we think it is, but also the young, shrill, now often tense voice of his daughter. Then we simply draw the curtain so nobody will see us listening. And we hear Netzer warning his daughter not to make such an exhibition of herself. Yes, father dear, she says, I'll be very quiet. For whatever he tells her or wants of her she always says—Yes, father dear. Or she says—Father dear, you're so kind, yes. Meanwhile he calls her his moth, as he had done earlier too. Sometimes we see— leaning especially far out then—a new doctor arriving, one of many he calls in for a lot of money, each time from farther and farther away, we see the doctor getting out of his car, holding his black bag, and looking for Netzer's apartment. Is that him? we hear her ask in her room upstairs. Yes, Netzer says, that'll be him. You can trust him, he's very experienced. But why is he so fat and red in the face, father dear? she asks, and just look at his fingers! How could such a fat red man find my soul? Hush, Netzer says, here he comes. Then we hear the new doctor stepping through the apartment and we imagine Netzer letting him into the room that none of us has seen. This time you'll be sure to answer all the doctor's questions, won't you? Prom-

2

ise? he says. Yes, father dear, she says. Then Netzer leaves her alone with the doctor and we imagine her sitting on a chair in the middle of her room, with her long brown hair, and the new doctor, her fourth or fifth, walking slowly around her. And we hear, too, the questions he asks, all having to do with her sickness, but she answers none of them, even though he pauses for a long time between the particular questions. He keeps asking: What did you have in mind when you took the match and started the fire, Fräulein Netzer? But she doesn't tell him. This doctor too, like her other ones, doesn't know how to cure her. All the same he behaves as if he'd found out what her sickness is, although, as he admits, not a trace of that sickness could actually be found in her. Yet she'll develop it later, he says and packs his tongue depressor away—to be on the safe side he's also looked into her throat. Then her father is back in the room and the new doctor, to do something at least, gives her an injection of pig serum, by which he sets some store. Then he leaves Netzer, with his daughter and her sickness, to his own devices.

Often when Netzer talks with her during the weeks that follow he refers to this sickness. Then he puts his arm around her shoulders and says— Tomorrow you'll be well again! She's also supposed to be clairvoyant. Once, when she was a little girl, she saw a hearse go by and called out: That's mama!—and true enough, her mother had run away from Netzer soon after that. His daughter too, after groundless attacks of anxiety, sometimes puts her arms around his neck and apologizes for being such a worry to him. But then you're really responsible for it all, she says, because you didn't make me strong enough for life. But how could I, Netzer exclaims—and him with his neck like a bull's from carrying halves of pigs around with him—how could I give you enough strength, when I haven't got any myself? He thinks her sickness is the result of a birthmark on her left cheek; it had troubled her a lot even when she was a child. Her mother, before having an operation to remove it, had had a similar birthmark on her right cheek. Sometimes Moth stays in her room for weeks on end, just because of this birthmark, she thinks that people will point at it, if she goes out on the street. In any case, ever since the fire—she might have burned the whole street down!—he won't be able to talk of her anymore as a sullen child who's oppressed by too many things, who only needs a change of air. (Considering the sullen child is a young woman of twenty-five with some tendency to corpulence, as we remind one another.) And he'd wanted to send her to a butcher friend of his in Rüdesheim on the Rhine, so that she'd be cured, but then it turned out that the friend had been divorced and had a second wife whom Netzer didn't know, and because of it all the friend had completely forgotten him and his daughter, so her Rhineland trip never came off. Instead, in front of Hübsch's cigar shop, nobody knows why, there's another scene, which we witness. We're leaning out of the window and can see quite distinctly how she clenches her fist and hits her father in the face with it. Without leaving the window we call out to other members of our family hidden in back rooms: Come and look, quick!—so that everyone will be able to see at least the second blow, but she doesn't hit him again. Instead, we see Netzer reaching for her left hand and gripping it, and he's telling her that he loves her. So of course we're disappointed. We'd hoped that the others would be able to see, them too, his daughter's madness that Netzer so obstinately denied, and now, instead, she's crying. His rimless glasses lie broken on the sidewalk and blood is running from his nose; he licks it away, so it won't drip onto his jacket. And the hat he wears, because of his thinning hair—so he wears it out of vanity, really—has fallen on the sidewalk and is rolling into the gutter. We see the wind pick it up and we shout—There it is, Herr Netzer! and we see him chasing the hat, with her running behind him. When he's caught up with the hat and dusted it off and put it back on his head, he comes over toward us, she has taken his arm and is walking beside him. Don't you know anymore what you promised me? he asks her. Yes, father dear, she says. And now see what you've done, he says and points up at us. Yes, father dear, she says. Then they're standing under our window and he speaks up at us. And says we mustn't get the wrong ideas about what we'd just seen, there's something hidden behind it. Yes, her madness, we shout, but Netzer shakes his head. Yet we'd seen her hit him. That's something he can't deny, we think, but we're mistaken.

Then—the weather has turned around, summer

is coming after all—Netzer is standing in his blue shirt smoking in front of his shop—his daughter walks up to him and supposedly whispers in his ear that all the men who've visited him during the past year in his sparsely furnished home—she has taken the best bits of furniture, we know—as soon as he'd left them alone with her for a briefest moment, had touched her and proposed indecent acts. Touched you! Netzer exclaims and he pulls her into their home at once, where? Here, she exclaims, on the sofa. And where did they actually touch you? he asks. Here, she says, and here! and she points to the places. Even Pastor Kant, this pious and quiet man, who, as we know from his wife, has been impotent for many years, no, has always been so, had tried to persuade her to commit indecent acts. Ah, Moth, Netzer says, and from now on he sends everyone who comes to talk to him straight back down the stairs. People who are really important for him he asks to visit him in the slaughterhouse. All, especially Pastor Kant, are of course deeply hurt and never forgive the Netzers. From that moment their life had little contact with the outside world.

Netzer thinks she might be cured, but we know otherwise, for across Mutschmannstrasse we hear their conversations, which are becoming more and more desperate, and what one of us doesn't hear, another does. Just look, father dear, she says, it's a fine life you've made for me. And when Netzer says: Shut up, Moth, for he'd wanted to make a quite different life for her, of course, and he can't stand the words "It's a fine life you've made for me," she

says—"Why mayn't I say it's a fine life you've made
for me?" And that she meant to be eternally grateful
for the way he pampered her. And that he must
promise to forgive her for having come to be the
way she is, but, well, under the circumstances, she
couldn't have come to be otherwise. Everything has
been leading that way, she says and she starts to
cry. Then Netzer thinks for a long time—we can
hear him thinking—and he walks around his daughter to see her once again from every side, and we
can hear his footsteps. But he can't think of anything to say and then both of them are crying.

One day she says—Father dear, if I ever get married, then I swear to you it won't be because I don't
love you anymore. You won't forget that, will you?
No, he says. Not ever? she asks. Not ever, he says.
Or she says—Shall I tell you what I want? I want
our garden to be a bit bigger. Or in the neighborhood to have a garden that's a bit bigger, which
needn't belong to me, but where I could walk around,
and I won't tear up the flowers at all. Yes, that's
what I want. You believe me, don't you? she asks.
Yes, I believe you, we hear him say. And then comes
a pause, and when it's over she says—Oh well, I'd
tear up the flowers anyway. If you'd rather put me
into an asylum, don't hesitate. But you must realize
that in an asylum I'll soon die, she says in that
forthright way which frightens her father so.

So he's crying again and we say—More and more
often he's crying. And we talk all the time about
him and his mad daughter. That's just before Netzer
got a prize from us for his meat and so was going

to be photographed by Herr Wilhelm, our photographer. In the evening we walk up and down outside his home; we hear our footsteps and we listen for hers above us, in the butcher's home. And we tell one another that he shouldn't go on refusing to admit that his daughter is mad, for he still refuses to admit it.

On the day Netzer is going to be photographed we run to Herr Wilhelm's photography shop and hope he'll soon come out. When he does so he is, just as we'd supposed, festooned with his equipment. We ask if he'll let us help him and take from him his tripod, the plates, and the heavy photographer's bag. Except he won't let us take the camera itself, a black box, because it has cost him a fortune and we might drop it. With the photographer between us, our arms full, we walk through our little town until we arrive at Netzer's place. We ring the bell and he comes down and opens the front door. Then he leads us up the stairs and lets us into his home. Unfortunately his daughter isn't there, and the door to her room, the room we want so much to see, is shut. Everything depends on the lighting, Herr Wilhelm says, and he takes two powerful lamps out of his bag. All the other things he needs we have to pass across to him, so he can assemble his apparatus. Netzer, who has never been photographed so expensively before, holds his Sunday hat in his hand and can't think of any way he might be helpful. Then Wilhelm tells him that he wants to make three studies of him. One sitting in the wicker chair, the second at the window with his butcher's flowers, and the third wearing his hat and standing by the wall, though he mustn't lean against it, "because, for such an active man as yourself, Herr Netzer, that would look too easygoing." But when Wilhelm points to the wicker chair—we're leaning against the opposite wall and won't be in the picture—Netzer says: Wait a moment! and he goes to his daughter's door and knocks and goes in, and we make as if to peer over his shoulder, eager as we are to see her room for once, but he puts his butcher's hands on our chests and pushes us back to the wall. And he goes back into his daughter's room and comes out with her in front of the camera and says that he won't be photographed without her, she belongs to him. Wilhelm, who has already switched on the two lamps and stuck his head under the black cloth, comes out again and looks at Netzer and his daughter. We look at them too, especially at the daughter, for we haven't seen her so close for a long time. She's put on a light-colored hat—or else her father has put it on her—and in such a low-ceilinged room a hat like that always makes a woman look comical. Also she's wearing—since we're so close we take a really good look at her—a light summer dress with short sleeves, which is oddly opposed to the sadness of her person. Delicate and spare as her bone structure is, her face and neck and body, probably because of the pig serum, are rather swollen, she looks as if she's been lying for a long time in a pond. Her name is Elisabeth, earlier she'd been called Elsi, we'll never forget that, and she's scared of us and doesn't look at us, whereas we stare at her incessantly, until she puts her hands over her face and says: Father! Father dear! Then Herr Netzer says to Herr Wilhelm, who insists on a single portrait and probably wouldn't have come for a double portrait: No, Herr Wilhelm, it can't be a single portrait. If you want to take a picture, it's got to be a family picture. A small family, I admit, he says and pulls his daughter, she resisting, across to face the camera, whereupon Herr Wilhelm winks at us from under his black cloth, because we all know that Herr Netzer's wife has left him and is now living in Berlin-Zehlendorf with a very rich manufacturer of flags, not married though, because Netzer hopes she'll come back and he refuses to get a divorce. Three studies are finally made that day. One in which father and daughter, side by side, hats on their heads, stand against the white living-room wall, as if they're in a shooting gallery; for the second she sits—after her father has calmed her down—in the wicker chair and looks up in admiration to her father standing over her; in the third both are sitting together on the striped sofa, she gripping his hand. But when he developed the pictures, Herr Wilhelm, who wants single portraits only, must have simply brushed the daughter out, for in the pictures hung a few days later in his shop window she isn't to be seen. In those pictures Netzer is smiling, not into his daughter's swollen face, but into vacancy.

That Sunday on which he has to commit her, our town is empty and silent. Finally he'll be rid of her, we say. But he doesn't want to get rid of her, shouts Herr Wilhelm, who's walking past at that moment—Netzer had gone and stood outside his shop and demanded an explanation for the missing daughter. So then he just doesn't know what's best for him, we say. No, Herr Wilhelm says, he doesn't want to get rid of her, and he remembers how Netzer got him by the collar and gave him a thorough shaking. Well, he doesn't know what he wants, we shout back. And we lean far out of the window and wonder why the taxi isn't coming. The asylum belongs to Dr. Augustin, who's familiar with her case, but she won't be staying with him. I've done what I could for her, Dr. Augustin says, but I'm an old man, the thing is out of my hands. Like other incurables in our area she'd be collected from his place and transferred to a central asylum. We didn't know what would happen to her there, but it wouldn't be anything good, she knew this herself, she wasn't as mad as all that. And more and more frightened she sits for hours at her window, looking in the direction of Dr. Augustin's madhouse. It has a high wall around it, to protect the world from her, but who'll protect her from the world? In any case we watch from our window and don't interfere, we just see the whole thing coming. But that's how it is in our town on the long August afternoons— dusty, straight, empty streets, yellow grass in the gardens, every house seeming empty, and even above the houses no air, no way out. Of course we'd rather leave the town, any day now war will be declared— we'd have liked to pass on through and out of the town, like the soldiers in the green troop carriers on the long road to Poland. But we can't leave our town, far from it, we'll live in this town forever, and probably die in it too. Just at that moment, when we'd stopped thinking about it, the taxi pulls up outside Netzer's home.

The driver gets out, walks around his taxi a few times, then he looks up at us.

The Netzers, he calls, do you know them?

We point at Netzer's front door.

The driver goes up to it and rings the bell, but nobody answers.

Shall we fetch them? we ask.

If you like.

We run quickly downstairs and out of our house and across the street. The street door to Netzer's home is unlocked. Because of our earlier visit we know his home and which is the door to it. Herr Netzer, your taxi's here, we call and we go up the stairs, aren't you ready yet? Herr Netzer, we call, fairly loud, in the entrance way to the roomy home which Frau Netzer had left so solitary. Then because nobody answers we press the door handle down and walk inside. The daughter's suitcase is packed and standing on the floor, except it's still open. We see her panties and her stockings and her brassiere. Herr Netzer, we call.

Then in the adjacent room, the daughter's room we've never seen, we hear some footsteps, also somebody seems to be sobbing. We press the handle down, but it won't budge. We put our ears to the door. Herr Netzer, we call. Then Herr Netzer says, impatiently—Just a moment, a moment!

But your taxi's here, we call, what's keeping you?

12

We're coming, Netzer says, what is it you want?

Nothing, we say, we don't want anything. Or is something wrong?

No, he says, it's nothing, I'll open the door in just a moment.

Then we hear a snap, another suitcase lock, we think, and that Moth will have a lot of luggage for her asylum, she won't need nearly so much. And since it's even hotter here than at our window, we take out our handkerchiefs, almost with a concerted movement, and mop our necks and foreheads with them. Then we hear the taxi honk, then we hear the bang.

We know at once that it isn't a pistol or rifle, a window slamming or a dropped book, but the humane killer from the slaughtery behind the house, where Netzer would sometimes slaughter a pig, and we hurl ourselves against the door. Even before we've broken it down, the second shot comes. Then the door gives way and finally we're able to see the room we've so often pictured to ourselves. Slowly our eyes move over the floor and the walls, even up to the ceiling and into a corner. And we see something we think we'll never in our lives forget, but which, all the same, in view of the carnage to come, we quickly did forget.

Casanova
and the Extra

I

In a recently discovered letter to the Portuguese ambassador Da Silva, the Prince de Ligne (1735–1814) writes concerning his friend Giacomo Casanova (1725–98), inter alia, that at a certain point in his life Casanova had an uncanny encounter, which would certainly have changed his life, if at that point his life could have been changed. For, he writes, Your Excellency must imagine that, after his escape from the Piombi and his banishment from Venice, constantly traveling and a refugee and somehow antagonized, frequent strong doses of distraction were his only means of rising above his condition. And immediately after his escape, one beautiful June day in Milan he has bought from an English major ruined by gambling a light well-sprung traveling coach and two powerful sorrel horses, and in this coach, behind these horses, he lives his life, as is well documented. Thus it was in this coach that he slept, after working a cleverly concealed mechanism which converted the ample seat into a bed, took his meals, mainly soups, composed his comedies, later his memoirs, or, every other day, with foam galore around his mouth, he shaved. (Naturally, too, having worked the same mechanism, he received his lady visitors.) For shaving, however, before he placed the razor to his throat, he also made the coachman stop; he'd become prudent, or, let's say, he'd learned his lesson. And then, it occurs to us, he always washed his hair—celebrated and discussed in all the courts of Europe—his brown curly hair, now of course rather scant and graying, mildewed, as people now remarked, washed it in this coach which, with its stiff linen curtains and black leather upholstery, has become his habitat. Yet he isn't old, and he's still healthy, though he easily tires, and nowadays, when he presents himself in the anterooms, bleary, but freshly shaved, and pays his compliments, he is sometimes hard pressed to conceal his despair at the constant changes which are leading him nowhere, especially since he isn't rich and he feels more and more drawn back to Venice. Yes, he feels drawn back to Venice nowadays, that's the main force in his life.

And now for the aforementioned uncanny encounter, which has an altogether involuntarily comic trait, and of which nobody else knows, but which

he himself told us about. An altogether unusual encounter of course, something altogether unique,
macabre too, yet moving, which occurred, unless
we're mistaken, on a hot August day in Geneva. In
his left coat pocket he has a letter of introduction,
already much crumpled and yellowed and brittle
at the folds, from a Count Bonafede of Parma, with
whom he shared, even in the same bed, fifteen or
twenty years before, his mistress at that time, Madame Podstoli. (He'd overlooked the fact that the
letter was still in his pocket.) Addressed to a Baroness Memma, who was reputed to have good connections with several Venetian business people. This
is what concerns him now. Thus, red-faced probably and slightly open-mouthed—he's run too fast—
he disposes himself approximately in the middle of
Memma's salon, with his legs spread somewhat apart
as usual (because of a minor ailment), he has made
his bow, not too deep (because of his pride), and he
introduces himself in his entirely correct but not
invariably intelligible French, in his customary way,
as follows: *I am Giacomo Casanova of Seingalt, I
come from Venice, a man of learning by inclination
and independent by habit. I travel for pleasure, I am
rich enough, I have no need to ask for anything. I ask
to be received.* Now, in this posture, he stands there
for a while. Excellent, excellent! But then something happened that had never happened before.
Suddenly it was announced that the baroness re-
gretted she hadn't the honor to know a Signor Casanova. What? She doesn't know him? But everybody knows him! Hadn't she been handed the letter

of introduction from Count Bonafede? exclaims Casanova, who is utterly perplexed, and twice with his cane, which has a silver pommel and which he has twice pawned, he strikes the floor.

Yes, she had, but she didn't know the count, either.

Then he'd like to ask if, nevertheless, the baroness would like to make his acquaintance. Tell her, he says and holds his head up, that I'm interesting. Tell her that throughout Europe my conversation . . .

His only belongings at that time: two coats, the better of which he's wearing. It is padded with wax-cloth at the crotch, as was the fashion in those days. In addition, some linen, much mended, not that one would see, five books, three of them attacking Voltaire, three snuffboxes, the aforementioned cane, a chain with a watch . . .

Well?

The baroness regrets, but she is with her husband, conversing.

2

A fair example of how he is antagonized by people. The world suddenly thinning out. Narrowing too. He's unwelcome in some places, people don't want to see him everywhere anymore. True, he still reaches out, but not everyone takes hold. But that wasn't what we meant to tell of, especially since the uncanny encounter didn't occur in Geneva. To judge by the tone, it could have been in Strasbourg. Yes, Strasbourg, that's where it was. Where, during the sixties, seventies, and eighties an attorney called Foscarini was living, a man who had good connections with several of the Venetian inquisitors . . .

Go quickly and tell the attorney, exclaims Casanova, who now supposes more and more definitely that his salvation consists in self-restraint and in a retreat from the wide open spaces of Europe, that, free man though I am, I've been traveling now for four days, unless I'm mistaken, almost without interruption, through remarkably bedraggled country, and now I'm tired, hungry too. Besides, I don't know anyone else here. And tell him it's dark as well, so we can't travel any further. And that our meeting is of the utmost importance.

To whom? the attorney's young servant will have asked.

To me, Casanova concedes.

So the servant goes to announce him.

Well? Casanova asks.

The attorney informs Signor Casanova that he's not at home, says the lackey.

Now one can hear from nearby, while the young and straight-limbed servant, not without jollity and warm interest, delivers this new injury, a small and not at all suppressed, indeed altogether hearty and unrestrained and freely ventilated burst of laughter. Casanova hears it, in any case. And since at this point in his career he still trusts his senses, he exclaims of course: But I can hear him laughing. That's the attorney's brother laughing, the servant explains, so that Casanova, who cannot possibly distinguish the attorney Foscarini from his brother by means of a laugh heard through two or three doors, and who can't prove anything, but has only a strong suspicion, once he has left Strasbourg again, toward midnight, deathly tired and dinnerless, curses to himself the indignity he's had to endure here . . . And because throughout his life he's felt himself to be a writer, if not a *poet* (we'll return to this later), he intends to write it all down at once, or in any case tomorrow, and to make public, possibly for posterity too, all the humiliation, all the disgrace, all the laughter, even laughter from behind closed doors, thus everything he's been subjected to in Strasbourg. And the next morning, in his light but well-sprung coach, he actually did take his quill from its case and, in verse, commit to paper some unfavorable and defamatory observations about this city, but then he could find no printer willing to publish them.

3

But to the point now, at last. The encounter that's supposed to be told of didn't occur in Strasbourg, as we see. We no longer know where it occurred. We only remember that he always wears, at about this time, one of those green coats which have sponges

in their armpits, because nowadays he often begins
to sweat. So often that he leaves more and more
frequently, with a brisk bow, the salons to which
he's still admitted and runs out, because the sponges
are full. Once outside, or else behind the stables, as
soon as he can't be seen, the sponges are wrung out.
The unhealthy fluids, you know, quickly into the
earth with them, downward. Meanwhile across his
chest he still wears those wide silver embroideries
which once shone so beautifully, but have now become quite black, further a yellow waistcoat, red
trousers—in brief, he still goes about as people went
about twenty years ago. Thus just as he was pictured in illustrations of his escape from the Piombi.
But he does this intentionally: Casanova always goes
about in the manner in which he has been depicted.
So that in the same fine costume, though it's aged,
dulled, and threadbare, he also implores in Ra-
venna a Mr. Gull from Brighton to help him get
back to Venice . . . And in the same fine costume,
though it's decrepit now, propped against the Leaning Tower of Pisa one morning, he wonders what's
happening to him. Why, you know, people throw
him out. And naturally he hits on the idea that he's
being slandered. But who are the slanderers? And
what have they brought into the world that has
been able to harm him so? Comes the time when
he can't see two heads close together without knocking them apart. Whenever people talk furtively now,
they're talking about him. And the quantity of fights,
but also of duels, in which he gets himself involved
nowadays, all serve the same purpose of fathoming

the matter. With this theory of slander he does himself much harm, of course. Not only does he get his collarbone broken, not only does he lose a tooth (and he's no longer got so many teeth to lose), also he antagonizes the friends he's still had till now. So that, if once he used to describe, traveling in his well-sprung coach, wide circles around Venice, he now needs (and is compelled) to describe increasingly narrower circles around Venice. He wants to be close to home, he wants to retrieve himself, diminish himself. And in Turin, where he only wants to try his luck at gambling (though he doesn't have much luck), he suddenly needs so badly to take a rest that, wearing the costume indicated above, with freshly wrung sponges, he sinks in the nearest anteroom onto the nearest chair, but this chair is then required nearby and is, in a manner of speaking, unnoticeably pulled away from under him. When Casanova realizes what has happened, he stands there for a moment, pale as a Pierrot; then he quits the anteroom and travels onward to Genoa.

4

Where he sits down—a heavy brown man, unequivocally ugly, but still quick-witted, or so he's convinced—in apothecary Belli's high, damp, and smoke-blackened kitchen. More things than rice are cooked in this kitchen. Belli is supposedly away on a trip (perhaps he is, but he needn't be, as Casanova has for some time been telling himself), so he sits

with the cook, Angela Caldi, who certainly isn't a
radiant beauty, but she's still young and firm-fleshed,
and he says: I've heard that the apothecary Belli
has three daughters, who are as beautiful as angels,
so when you sit in church with them, that makes
four angels in the church. And he pays her other
compliments, like: Come and sit on my knee! Or:
Come on, open your blouse, show me your breasts!
And then, as always: *Because I'm Casanova of Venice, always on my travels.* And for my pleasure, he
adds, I'm traveling to Paris tomorrow, and, if you
like, little one, we'll travel together. But young Caldi
only giggles, doesn't show him her breasts, doesn't
sit on his knee, but leans somewhat nonplussed
against the heavy dark table, which is overloaded
with capons that have to be plucked by tomorrow;
and the presence of this grotesque and overripe man,
inscrutable as he is, and a stranger to kitchens, who
has put a clove in each nostril because of the smell
of dead birds, perplexes and troubles her. Not even
in the kitchen now is there a trace of the magic he
once exuded in the salons. One merely giggles and
feels uneasy, but he's heavy and doesn't notice this.
I've always loved women, he says, who stammer
and blush. But you, Angela, are much better. You
giggle, he says, and say nothing. And since it's a
dismal day and what lies ahead of him is dismal
too (the journey to Paris, *without any money*), he
places his rheumatically knotted fingers on her warm
breast . . . For on this dismal day in this cool kitchen
he has a craving for warmth, for intimacy, he wants,
if possible, to be consoled by her, or distracted at

least. He craves for feelings, too, because he has realized: You don't feel anything anymore, for months, if not years, you've hardly felt anything, you've got to have feelings again! The kitchen maid's full breasts, even while she's plucking capons, might perhaps have deflected from him the apprehension (we won't call it fear yet) that he might never feel anything again. But then the girl, who spends her nights with the cook and has no wish for other caresses, calmly pushes away his hand and the mouth with the greedy tongue in it, as well as the long dark member, altogether slack, like a piece of pigskin, which this gentleman with a lech for tenderness quite unexcitedly pulls, by way of further argument, out of his red trousers, and she moves to the other side of the table. True, with his trousers open Casanova scuttles after her for a while, but he doesn't get to her, he only lunges into the capons. Listen, he says and wants to make his *confession* to her, as he does to all the others. You are, he exclaims, the only one I could love and for whom, he exclaims, I was always looking. Even the freest man in the world, he exclaims, would renounce for her his independence. Only she shouldn't cower like that behind the table, behind those capons, which could surely wait a bit, in view of his feelings? His head, if not between her legs and on her breast, at least on her shoulder, wouldn't she just . . . To rest it, he exclaims, only to rest it. And to touch, he exclaims, if not your breasts and your neck, and not your shoulders either, then at least to touch your hand. *I need something*, don't you understand? A pity, he says when young Caldi doesn't even let him take her hand, but instead pushes it into a capon, at this moment in my life a little proximity might have . . .

5

So to Paris, he goes there alone, and the encounter . . . Well, we'll see. In Paris, having secured for a few sous a space for his coach behind the Hotel Moor, he closes the linen curtains on both sides. And employs the next four hours grooming himself, restoring by art the natural charm he's been deprived of by changed circumstances. First he shaves, then he puts on a lace shirt, then, after fastening dry sponges in his armpits, he slips into the better one of his coats, all in this cramped coach. And then in the coach he dresses his long, though thinning and altogether lackluster hair. Then he powders his hair, and finally, having lined his eyebrows, he makes his eyelids up. And he doesn't forget to place a big clove under his tongue. In the salon of Countess d'Urfé, widow, fifty-six, but very rich, he and she *face-à-face*, he and she in their grandest attire, Casanova—the conversation exhausts him even before it has begun—tries to hide his exhaustion behind an air of liveliness, rapidly assumed, and, to the lady's feeling, rather fishy. He makes thus his bow and seats himself, but his movements are much too polished and debonair for his present circumstances. And now for the conversation.

Casanova: From Venice, independent, a free man. And he bows, despite his pride, an adroit and deep bow, so as to show the countess the mobility of his large and ponderous body, the joints of which are becoming more and more terminally stiff. (A stiffness foreshadowing rigor mortis.)

Whereupon Countess d'Urfé, she doesn't say why, but she wants to see him from behind. Turn around, turn around, turn around, she exclaims and claps her hands.

Casanova isn't sure about the impression he makes from behind, but, with apprehension, he turns around.

Fine, she says—and Your Excellency had best read very fast what follows. For it's akin to comedy and perhaps beneath our dignity. Yet at Casanova's time of life he does involuntarily play in comedies, and we've no wish to pass over the fact. Fine, she says thus, and now once more from the front. Fine, so once more from the front! What a peculiar nose you've got, the countess exclaims. And in these large brown Venetian eyes there's something, she says, that interests her. What might it be?

My powerlessness, Casanova guesses.

That, she says, might be so. Let's talk about it.

I'm not thinking of asking you for money, Casanova replies.

So he has some?

No.

Is he looking for a position with her? And when he answers in the affirmative the countess asks: And how do you propose to earn money from me?

He could, Casanova says, go riding with her every morning.

She'd stopped riding long ago.

He could, he suggests, be her secretary.

I've got one.

Educate your children?

They've been grown up for a long time, d'Urfé says, though they are uneducated.

I could entertain you.

How?

With my conversation. In all Europe, says Casanova and straightens himself in his chair, I'm renowned for my conversation, and my knowledge, he says, has been called encyclopedic, by my adversary Voltaire.

She: Is that so?

What's more, he says, this isn't just dry knowledge, he's intelligent, witty. He means: Under appropriate circumstances he could very easily be intelligent, witty.

And what would you be witty about with me?

I could acquaint you with the latest things in science, Casanova says, and we apologize for the farcical turn their conversation is about to take.

No, she says, no science.

Casanova and the Extra

Poetry?

No, she says, no poetry.

I could tell you stories about my life.

For instance?

How I escaped from the Piombi.

I know that already, d'Urfé says, I once read about it.

So, no conversation. And after a moment's silence: A pity that my age and appearance don't allow me to . . .

And Casanova: Your age, what do you mean?

So you don't find me old? she asks.

Madame is at the peak of her beauty.

You think so?

Madame makes upon me . . . Casanova assures her and now he even places his hand on his heart, and once more we ask to be forgiven if this miserable but on both sides deeply serious conversation turns into a farce or has already done so. Anyway the rich old woman apparently still makes a desirable impression on the poor old man. And, he adds, he's not so young anymore, either.

But still vital?

And Casanova, after a moment of self-scrutiny: More often than not, yes.

And I wouldn't be repugnant to you, but would excite your vitality?

27

And Casanova again: Not repugnant. Excite. Yes. No. Yes.

Well then, says the countess, who suddenly, contrary to all reason, contrary also to all experience, starts to hope she might have overhastily reconciled herself to the decline of her charms and that the dark colossus in her chair might really still be able to descry, through what she thought had declined, something exciting and desirable: Well then, she says, perhaps you're right. In that case she could find for him a position with the lottery, he wouldn't have to do much. She'd set up a house for him, coach and horses, of course. Servants . . . Evenings he could go to the opera, the ballet. He could, in God's name, keep a mistress too, if he wanted, that wouldn't trouble her, just so long as the aforementioned vitality stayed fresh and vigorous. But you'd be obliging me, monsieur, she says, if in spite of my appearance, or seeing through my appearance, you'd once or twice a week . . . a night in your arms. And again, hopefully: Yes, perhaps she'd only imagined that she was old and that it was all over. For it really wasn't long since she'd been young. She could still clearly remember how her husbands were always around her and the mere sight of her foot had sent them into raptures. This foot here, she says and sticks it out.

What a pretty foot, Casanova exclaims and he takes up the position of a man spellbound with admiration. Any moment, in his economic straits, he'll pounce, as it were voraciously, on the old leg. Prob-

ably he now meant to kiss the foot, in any case he
leaps up, but makes a false step, and without actually falling down and becoming drastically pros-
trate, simply because of the false step, please forgive
us now, he *damages his own foot* so calamitously
that, the conversation being concluded (here the
farce ends), he can't stand up anymore, but, with
melting hair (the pomade!), blackened cheeks (the
makeup!), armpits dripping (the sponges with the
fluids!), he is lifted by two strong serving men onto
a sort of litter (we'd rather not call it a stretcher)
and carried out of the room, down the stairs and
to his coach, well aired in the meantime, behind
the Hotel Moor, pushed into the coach and, after
the cleverly concealed mechanism has been worked,
deposited there. And for the time being he can as-
sume no position at the lottery or anywhere else,
but . . . But here we'll let the matter drop and say
only this much, that this too wasn't *the encounter*.

6

Paris therefore, at the flower market, in the morning. Ask anyone walking there—Why are you here?
and he'll say—It's because I want to see these carts
swaying under their cargoes of fruits and flowers.
Because I'd like to take in more deeply the fra-
grances of nature. Yet everyone knows that the only
people who visit the market are men and women
who have passed the night together, or haven't slept
at all because of despair or pain. This is where the

wrinkled pants and dresses are displayed. Here, at the Paris flower market, even in the early morning, it's the done thing to be limp and exhausted. And this is where Casanova has been coming for a time, after lonely nights, limp and exhausted, to pass by the fruits, borne on his litter, and, once or twice a week, to smell the flowers with astonishment.

7

And then in Padua the machine. But in Padua he's quite close to his native town and if he stands on the hills he can see Venice before him. His cloak drawn tight around him, hat pressed down over his forehead, he stands leaning against his coach and believes he can see before him, tangible, rising out of the mist of ordinariness, the domes and towers of which he's always dreaming nowadays. And even the gigantic but graceful palace with the Bridge of Sighs, so he later maintains, even this, on a cloudy spring day, quite distinctly, from Padua . . . For when he arrives Padua is dismal, the sky sultry and pallid, now and then a misty rain falls, yet when I draw breath, he thinks, I breathe the air of home.

In Padua Casanova installs his coach behind the Dove Hotel. Then, even before he can open his suitcase and take his wig out, a messenger from the municipal court hands him a summons. At the court he's made to wait. So he has time to walk up and down the long corridors and to discover in a corner a machine that's usually covered by a cloth, but the cloth has been removed for him and we have to imagine the machine looking like this: It has the shape of a very large horseshoe, with a stool in the center of it. And having nothing else to do he sits on the stool. Buckles and straps hang around him now like greedy tongues. And then suddenly someone is standing beside him explaining the machine to him, and the explanation runs roughly as follows: If anyone is not welcome in Padua, he's made to sit on this stool and his head is turned so that this piece of iron here (pointing at the horseshoe) firmly grips his neck. And this silken cord, which unwinds from the machine, as if automatically, is then conducted, in the open half of the horseshoe, across the unwelcome person's throat, like this. The ends of the cord run to the axle of this wheel (the wheel, too, is pointed out to him), to which they are then fastened, and then someone turns the wheel, very slowly. (But the wheel isn't being turned, not yet it isn't.) Until, without actually being forced, the person who's unwelcome in Padua, which is very close to Venice and entirely under its influence, is very slowly, very slowly . . .

This machine is one of the most perfect devices I've ever set eyes on, Casanova says. Are you the one who turns the wheel?

And he gets off the stool and goes back to the Dove, and, without opening his suitcase and taking out his wig, which is full of holes anyhow, he gets back into his coach and, never having spoken to the magistrates, who have nothing to say to him anyway, travels on to Ferrara, where for three days he succumbs to gambling. When he's asked, during the course of a conversation among gentlemen, which part of a woman's body means most to him, he replies: The neck. And he gives the following reasons: The neck is the link between head and heart. Not for nothing are gold and silver hung around the neck. And whenever he places his hand on a woman's neck he can distinctly feel that she's alive. Also the neck arouses wishes that are not short-lived and coarse, but subtle and enduring. For not only do words flow through the neck, not only does mind, that is, but also air does, even when no words are being spoken. When the lady has gone to sleep, he says, I've always looked for a long time at her neck, which always has been very vulnerable. And as he is speaking, he grasps his neck.

8

And then Rome, the Vatican, and finally, or not, the *unparalleled encounter*. And here we introduce, in extract, a conversation between Giacomo Casanova of Venice and Pope Clement XIII of Venice, which is supposed to have occurred in the gardens of the Quirinal Palace, as follows:

Casanova, pathetically or desperately: Like an insect which has crept around at your feet for a while and now has to be trodden on . . .

Casanova and the Extra

The Pope, very old: Yes, I remember. Your appeal. You'd like to go back to Venice?

Then Casanova exclaims with great emotion: Yes, Holy Father!

And yet you ran away.

Yes, Casanova says, but now I must go back, or I'm lost. When I was younger I had adventures that helped me not to feel lost, but now I must go back.

Then the Pope says: Come closer, Giacomo, I'll tell you something in confidence. And in a whisper: Do you see those people in black robes over there beside the pond where the bushes are? They'd like to slip me their appeals too, they've been waiting for years. You must realize they're all exiles. They come from all sorts of different countries, but all came to me for the same reason, for the same reason as you. They all suffer from that terrible malady. They all suffer from homesickness. But how can I help them? It's a sickness our forefathers knew and described. *Nos patriae fines et dulcia linguimus arva.* Let's go to my ponds, he later says. Let's look at my swans. But, as you perhaps don't realize, I have a bad leg and have to be carried, how lamentable, because, look, the ponds are so near. And he seats himself, or rather lets himself be installed, in his red sedan chair and gives a sign to the musician who is supposed to follow them. So we have to imagine the following conversation being conducted to the rhythm of a sedan in motion and, at its oddest moments, brought to a climax by the notes of a violin.

Perhaps, says Casanova, who speaks first, perhaps I shouldn't have run away when I did.

There are swans here, aren't there, the Pope replies, who probably doesn't see so well anymore.

Yes, Your Holiness, says Casanova, who in his excitement had overlooked the swans entirely.

Then get some bread, Giacomo, and feed them! Throw them big soft chunks.

I oughtn't to have run away, Casanova continues while he feeds the swans, majestic and pure in their motions, but which he hadn't anticipated, I shouldn't have escaped from the Piombi.

Yes, the Pope says, they say you tell a good story, especially the one about your escape. No, tell me first how you were arrested.

It was during the night before July 25, 1755, Casanova tells him. I was young. I had misbehaved, and now I had to be punished for it. But instead of accepting the punishment I ran away. But now I'd like to go back, and they won't let me.

And that's all, the Pope asks.

Yes, Casanova says.

Well now, you're really not such a good storyteller as they've been saying, says the Pope after a while from the soft corner of his sedan. You make a big mistake. You don't tell events in sequence, that way you'll never enthrall me. One always has to tell stories one thing at a time, as you at your age ought to know, but you try to present everything at once, probably because you're so confused in yourself.

Casanova and the Extra

The best thing would be for you to start again from the beginning and describe to me, first, the debaucheries you gave yourself up to in those days. Isn't it true that you lived a life of debauchery?

Yes, Casanova says, I was living a terrible life, but there are worse things. Except in those days I didn't know what the worse things were.

You're confusing everything again, the Pope says. You should tell me about your debaucheries, not about your penitence.

Will you support my appeal, if I tell you about my debaucheries? Casanova asks.

First tell me, the Pope says, but one thing at a time, and in detail. Then we'll see.

But the story of my debaucheries is long, Casanova says, if I tell it in detail and systematically.

All the better, the Pope says.

And if, Holy Father, Casanova exclaims, if you don't help me, shall I to the end of my days have to . . .

The debaucheries, Giacomo, the debaucheries, the Pope exclaims.

But Holy Father, Casanova says, I do repent of them. Can't anyone see that I do? I'm a different person now.

Have you got married? the Pope asks.

Marriage, Casanova says, that's difficult.

So you haven't got married?

No.

But do you want to get married? Yes, that's a great and worthy enterprise, says the Pope and yawns.

If I got married, Casanova asks, would you make it possible for me to go back?

An enterprise, the Pope says, that needs to be carefully considered.

So I'd better not get married? Casanova asks.

And the Pope: I see you've got tired, Giacomo. Like me. The burden of our years and our activities has exhausted and weakened us both.

Yes, Casanova says, but you haven't yet told me what I'm supposed to do. Whether I should get married or not get married. Allow me to kiss your slippers while you're thinking about it.

By all means, by all means, the Pope says.

And Casanova, when the sedan has come to a halt, as he kneels down and, through the curtain, kisses unhurriedly two embroidered slippers: My humility has no bounds. Like my penitence. But I need advice, I need help.

Yes, the Pope says, I really ought to help you now.

Yes, Casanova exclaims, help me! Tell me what to do. And with his face turned to the ground, eyes closed: I'm listening! And when no answer comes, again: I'm listening, I'm listening. And when the silence above him remains unbroken, he looks up, but the curtain through which the Holy Father has been speaking to him is drawn. And when he asks one of the attendants what has become of the Holy Father, he's told: He has fallen asleep.

9

So let's make plans! Come, give me your hand! We'll
settle down and go on our way together, from now
on. The great riddles of nature and human life, we'll
solve them together. I, my little . . .

Anna, she says.

. . . my little Anna, he says, will continue my search
for the great philosophical truths, and you will look
for the little ones, the truths of everyday life, they're
the loveliest of all. Would you be able to love me?

Thus Casanova, well over fifty, but who'd like to be
loved, yet what is still lovable about him?

He has asked this question of himself now and has
investigated each and every outer and inner trait,
without hitting on any answer. All the same: Would
you be able to love me? Thus Casanova, between a
pigsty and a stable, one foot in a puddle. Would
you . . . ?

Like a father!

10

Thus the kitchen maid Anna Pocchini beside the
stable behind the Steadfast Saint hotel in Bologna,
where his light coach now stands. But this wasn't
the uncanny encounter. He flings himself down again
amid the black upholstery, but just when his coachman is about to turn aside to water the horses the

way is blocked. Uh-oh, a nasty surprise! Uh-oh, a funeral procession! And then Casanova, in his hurry to quit the place of his humiliation, makes a crass mistake. For he leans out of the window as far as he can and shouts to the coachman: Drive on! Drive on! And as a result, through his impatience, through his impetuousness, he becomes involved, together with his oft-described coach, in the funeral procession. True, he leans at once out of the window again, even further, if that's possible, and gives the coachman even louder and more urgent commands to extricate them from the funeral procession and change direction, even if it means going the opposite way, but because the street is so narrow the coachman can't escape and is simply swept along. Where? To the graveyard, of course.

11

Which you must think of like this: Still alive in the midst of death, Casanova sees to the left through his coach window suddenly tall pines and dark cypresses, figures lurking beneath them, angelic stone, transfigured already. Meanwhile from in front a white chapel is slowly being pushed toward him. And the horses drawing the hearse, which is just ahead of him, have golden reins, black and white plumes. And Casanova looks from his window corner and scans the procession, the clothes people are wearing, the faces they are making. Now they turn onto a muddy and damp side path, with roots and rocks, he's afraid that the hearse ahead of him will keel over, that the coffin might crash to the ground, and he imagines, compulsively, you understand, its rigid cargo, which he thinks of in horror as a man the same age as himself, also of his stature and with his features, rolling out of the burst coffin. And *then* he sees himself lying on the ground, in his better coat. Entire cartloads of corpses in the ground here—and you'd be a liar to deny it. As for the coat, he imagines the top button isn't buttoned up, which looks very slovenly. Because even a Casanova can't tell whose hands he might fall into, should he ever die, and what coat he'll be stuck into, and if it'll be buttoned up at the top. But keep moving, keep moving!

But because they can't move and the procession is slowing to a halt, Casanova now has time to make one more mistake. Outraged, because he doesn't wish to be where he is, he flings open the coach door, to escape from the coach, and is immediately swept along by the stream of mourners, into which he stumbles, and he lands up beside a fresh grave. So there wasn't only a funeral procession, there was a burial too! But so far he doesn't know who's being buried, doesn't even know where, inside the coffin, the head is and the feet are. (But he doesn't want to know, either.) Then comes a short and serious conversation with the gravestone to his left, as it suddenly shifts very close to him. I'm Casanova, independent, Casanova exclaims and stands straight up. And the gravestone replies, cringing: Once we were just like you. Anyway the pallbearers now hoist up, head or feet foremost, the coffin, which is only a box painted black. And where do they carry the coffin to? To the open grave, of course, whither Casanova has been pushed and where he's waiting for the box. Which is now placed on the dirt practically at his feet, while the pallbearers pull their rope through beneath the coffin and position themselves on either side of the pit. Then, naturally, since he doesn't belong here and is feeling quite out of place, Casanova wants most of all to step away from the grave, but naturally, too, he doesn't want to antagonize the corpse. And besides, he's hemmed in, he's hemmed in.

So now for the burial. After the box has been given over to God and prayed at and blessed on its way, it is lowered into the dirt by the pallbearers, being of no more use to anyone, while the rope, which can still be used, is quickly pulled up again. The open, black, comfortless pit remains, and the emotional, hatless and joyless mourners now throw respectively dirt or flowers into it. Will Casanova be throwing flowers? No, Casanova won't be throwing anything: Casanova, whose mortality isn't proven, especially since he has many plans and there's much all around for him to see and feel and enjoy. Then come the gravediggers, into whom the pallbearers have transformed themselves, and suddenly with shovels in their hands they're standing over the grave pit and tossing dirt onto the box, and being forgotten begins.

Before coming back to the comedy, which this tragedy is, and describing Casanova's walk from the
side paths and his return to the main path and to
his coach, we must mention the gray rat he met
under the oleander bush on his way back. A fat,
fleshy, damp animal which doesn't scare but takes
his measure, as it were, with popping red eyes and
trembling tail and bared teeth. In the graveyards
of this region there are millions of rats like this one,
unnoticeably busy and at home in their tunnels which
ramify far and wide under the earth's crust. And
they're waiting, Casanova thinks, and he returns
the stare and puts a hand on his dagger. Then the
animal slips away. But, uncanny as it was, this too
wasn't the encounter.

Meanwhile he starts to brood. Why did the coachman have to water the horses just when the funeral
procession was coming by? Why not a few minutes
earlier? Or later? Or by another road? Had fate
wished it so? But then he'd be a fatalist! No, thinks
the philosopher in Casanova, for in that case you'd
have, for the honor of your system, to believe in the
connectedness of all events, and then there'd be no
freedom left for you. And he rejects fatalism, because he wants to be a free man and no part of a
machinery, even if the latter encompassed heaven
and earth. Thus for reasons of vanity. But why at
that precise moment did his coach . . . This frightens
him, startles him. So that, walking now toward the
graveyard gate and soon out of the graveyard, he
takes a deep breath and thinks: Life! Life! Life! In

fact a woman, a resolutely breathing being, a young widow perhaps, something warm and giggling and firm-fleshed, who must be hereabouts and, like him, needs comfort and could bring him back to life. And he's already walking behind a woman who seems to come out of the bushes into which the rat vanished and to possess one of those ample but firm behinds which he prizes so highly. And she's even really clad in black, and, after passing through the gate and crossing the street, she's about to vanish inside the Steadfast Saint hotel.

Madam!

The lady turns round: Giacomo!

Mother! Ah, it's you, Casanova exclaims in quite a different voice, and as if something had bitten him he pulls away the arm he was going to put around her waist.

Yes, it's me, the old woman says.

12

Yes, this is it. The uncanny encounter we wanted to tell of, because it could have changed Casanova's life, if his life at this point . . . With his mother, of course, in Bologna! Whom he hasn't seen for years, even decades. To be honest: He hadn't reckoned with her because he thought she was dead, supposing, that's to say, like everyone else that she'd died of smallpox in Dresden about thirty years before. But since his mother is standing there before him now, well, then she won't have died after all, he thinks, but must somehow have survived the smallpox. And because of the strong emotions which will assail them any moment now, they can't very well stay on the street, a bit of a wind has arisen and it's disarranging their hair, so together they abruptly enter the Steadfast Saint, where his mother, so she says, has been lodging for the past few days in a little room up under the roof, whereas his little coach down in the courtyard, as we know, is . . .

And now Your Excellency has to imagine your way, in a cheap hotel, into a very cheap, thus very shabby hotel room. Casanova stands at the door and asks if he may go in. Go right on in, his mother exclaims in a rather hoydenish manner that she never had before, and it disconcerts him a bit. And when he hesitates she even pushes him inside, vehemently too, with both hands. So here's the room, dark and cramped, though it's almost empty. Also it hasn't been aired. Nobody will clean up for her and of course she's too frail to do it for herself, so he thinks, with shame, and he decides that before leaving and getting back into his coach he'll clean the room once at least, and especially the thick eiderdown, from which an awful smell seems to be coming, he'll carry it to the window and give it a really good shake.

And now for the conversation, which did perhaps occur, or could have occurred, in this attic room, cramped and stuffy, high up in the house, but low-ceilinged, that late autumn afternoon on which Casanova had actually been meaning to leave, only to land up in the graveyard. Being more self-possessed and less surprised and not so breathless, besides she's already sitting on the sofa, his mother is the first to speak. Sit down, Giacomo, she says, why are you so out of breath?

It's been quite a surprise, Casanova says, and he sits down in an armchair that's much too narrow for him; quickly he fans a little air at himself with an embroidered silk handkerchief. What brings you so suddenly to Bologna, Mama?

Chance.

Just like me, Casanova says. I'm only here by chance too.

Yes, but a different chance.

That's true, Casanova says, and that's not all. Just think, just as we met I'd been wondering for a long time about the equivocal and elusive nature of the concept, chance, which probably isn't a concept at all. For if you look more closely at the matter, my chance consisted of a series of connected necessities. Actually I'm here by necessity.

And why do you think I'm here, his mother asks. Are my connections fewer?

No, no, Casanova exclaims—he doesn't want to annoy or offend his mother, who's apparently not only very small, but also very sensitive, right at the beginning of their encounter. But it's by chance that we finally did meet, isn't it? he asks.

You always did talk nonsense, she says.

44

Others would say I talk like a philosopher, says Casanova and straightens himself somewhat, as best he can, in his narrow armchair. Also he now puts his handkerchief away, he's done enough fanning. Now a clumsy attempt at tenderness, because he thinks it's expected: He stands up and walks over to her and, so as to kiss her on the cheeks, means to take her head between his fleshy red hands, which he'd thrust under the Pocchini girl's skirt a while ago.

Don't be silly, you're sweating all over, she exclaims and pushes him away. And how heavy you've got, you can hardly breathe. Altogether you seem to me in a poor state. Can you still touch your toes?

You live too high up, Mama, Casanova says, for such an . . .

For such an old woman, his mother exclaims and she laughs. You're welcome to speak your mind. I know it anyway. Yes, the heart! All hearts! Yours, too. They're machines, as an apothecary was explaining to me the other day, except these machines have veins and sinews instead of pistons and wheels. Your heart-machine is in a poor state. You've let it slide.

Ah, a little fresh air and I'll be all right again, Casanova says. Best thing would be if I open the window. And draw back this thick curtain here, at last, he adds, because he'd like to let a little light into the darkness of the room and at last be able to see his mother properly. Noontime, he thinks, and so dark still, really she's letting herself slide! And so he walks to the window and pulls back the curtain and opens the window and sticks his congested head out and draws a few breaths, but when he and his head are back in the room again it's still dark, so he still can't see his mother clearly. True, he sees her sitting on the sofa, but particular features are very vague. For instance, it's quite impossible for him to see what sort of a face she's making. To judge by the angle of her head, she could even have nodded off.

Yes, says his mother, so she isn't asleep, and now you're disenchanted. You thought I was a young woman when you came clambering after me. One to refresh yourself with, while your horses guzzle their water.

Mother, Casanova exclaims, outraged, from the open window.

For, as I hear, his mother says, you're supposed to have developed into a great connoisseur of our sex. Now, take my gloves off! And then, when he kneels before her and kisses her hands: Yes, those are very old hands. Smooch away, smooch away! I suppose you've never kissed old hands like these? Right, that's enough, stop it now. Are you crying?

It's the surprise, Mama, after these many years, says Casanova who actually has shed a few tears.

Do you know how many years it is? she asks. And when Casanova is silent: So you've forgotten that, too. It's thirty-three years since you saw me, Giacomo. Thirty-three years. *I* haven't forgotten. *I* have counted the years.

Mother, Casanova exclaims, suddenly sorry about it all.

And you've never in your life asked after me, and finally you didn't even *think* of me anymore, because your head was so full of other women. And when, in spite of it all, I sometimes did make myself noticeable, you simply killed me, if only in your head. You simply persuaded yourself that she's dead, the old woman, and right away you buried her in your thoughts. Then you wouldn't have to think of her anymore, it was too much for you. And now you're crying, because you've got a guilty conscience. And you're surprised, of course.

Mother, Casanova exclaims.

Because I'm not dead, his mother suddenly exclaims far too loud, and to prove it she strikes her knee with her fist a few times. Do you hear that I'm not dead? Before I die I'd like to have one more talk with you, she says and she moves deeper into her sofa corner. And because she's come to be so small and thin, her son thinks she must be cold, and he tries to spread a little black blanket, which he chanced to find on the windowsill, across her knees, but she pushes him away. What are you doing, she exclaims. Haven't I told you I'm not dead yet? Here, you'd better hold my wool!

And she pulls knitting needles and a ball of black wool out of her spacious black handbag, which is studded with black pearls.

You're going to knit now? Casanova exclaims.

Yes, a shirt, she says. Does that make you wonder, perhaps? If I don't knit it quickly now, who'll knit it *then*? And I don't want to arrive empty-handed.

Arrive where?

So what have you got to tell me after these many years, says his mother, evading the question—during the time he hasn't seen her she must have become altogether expert and reckless in her relations with men.

Yes, what have I got to tell her, Casanova thinks. How energetic she still is and how well she speaks! For unlike other old people Casanova has known, even if only fleetingly (he's always avoided them), his mother pronounces every single word clearly and quite intelligibly, and the sense of the words is true as well, though sometimes a bit cloudy. And she isn't the least bit moved to have met him here. She doesn't even seem to be surprised. You're still a beautiful woman, Mama, he says. You still have . . . beautiful eyes.

Yes, she says, that's what they've told me, too—that you always pay women compliments and tell them what they want to hear. Because you think it'll help you with them, to reach your goal more rapidly. As for you, you're no longer as young as I've always imagined you to be.

Well, Casanova exclaims, when all is said and done I'm . . .

I know how old you are, his mother says. But unfortunately you look even older, much older. Because you don't stand up straight. A man of your height and your figure ought to stand up straight.

It's because I . . .

Worries weigh on you?

Yes.

We'll talk of that later. In any case, worries or not, you must stand straight up, or else you'll be a humpback a year hence. Then people will chase after you in the street to touch your hump, because that supposedly brings good luck and riches, but I doubt if it does. That's to say, if you're still alive.

A year hence?

Who knows? And what's become of your beautiful hair, his mother suddenly exclaims out of the darkness of her corner. You're quite bald on top already. Did you lose it all at once or bit by bit?

Bit by bit.

And what do you do about it? I hope you don't simply watch it happening, but do something about it.

I have . . . various remedies.

Do you rub them into your skull?

I take them.

You swallow them?

Yes.

And how do they taste?

Horrid.

Horrid, she exclaims and gives a loud laugh and then even slaps her knee again (and if she weren't his mother you might think she was gloating). And probably they aren't even the right remedies, for plainly they don't help, she exclaims. Listen, if I don't forget I'll give you *my* remedy. That does help. I've been using it for forty years now. Look at my hair, see how thick it still is.

Yes, Mama, he says, it's still thick.

Feel it, if you like, so you won't one day reproach me for deceiving you, his mother says and she bows her head slightly.

Yes, it's still thick and full, Casanova says and he walks up to her and lightly strokes her hair, which, probably because it's still so full, repulses him somewhat, because it's not right that his mother's hair should be so full while his own . . . You really are my mother, aren't you? he asks and he stoops toward her, meaning to look her finally in the face, but then his mother simply extends her arm and simply pushes him away from her.

Yes, yes, she says, I'm your mother all right.

I was only asking, Casanova says and he resolves not to give in this time and not to let himself be pushed away by her, but then she simply takes the long and sharp disengaged needle and sets it at his throat, so that going closer to her is unthinkable.

What are you doing, he exclaims and draws back.

I'm playing with you, she says.

And what if you hurt me, he asks.

That doesn't matter, she says, you're big and strong now, and besides, I'm only tickling you a bit.

I only asked if you are my mother, he says, because in Dresden that time, you remember . . .

Yes, she says, a few people did die.

I still remember, Casanova says, how the news came, that you too . . .

Yes, she says, but it was falsified.

Curious, he says, who'd falsify that kind of news?

How should I know, she exclaims, one always has enemies. And besides, she says, the whole affair was so long ago that there's nothing to be gained from talking at length about it.

Yes, he says, but at that time it did . . .

Surprise you, his mother asks.

It shattered me, Casanova exclaims.

Well now, his mother says, you soon got over it, so people told me.

Yes, it's true, Casanova thinks. And then, after a short interval, he wants finally to concentrate his thoughts, but what on? I only asked, he says, if you're my mother because you've changed so much.

And how have I changed?

I mean, Casanova says—but fear about these changes that have overlaid her earlier gentleness and warm-heartedness and have brought to the surface a con-tentiousness and self-righteousness, which she probably used to hide with the utmost care, pre-vents him from explaining what he meant. Besides, these changes are too subtle, in their particulars, to be encompassed in a few words forming a sentence, however long the sentence might become. Best let the matter drop, he thinks, and say something quite different, she won't notice anyway. But because he can't think of anything else to say either, he decides to say simply the opposite of what he'd been meaning to say. I meant, he therefore says, that you actually haven't changed *at all* since the last time. But of course this isn't true. For even outwardly, as one can see, too, at an arm's length and in the darkness, in spite of her hair, which is still thick, his mother has changed profoundly. For instance, to name only the most important feature, she's much smaller than she used to be.

Yes, she's says, you're right. I haven't changed much. I've still got much more hair than you and yet I'm so much older. Now show me your teeth!

Oh God, Mama!

Aha, she exclaims, as for that you haven't got many left. That's why your cheeks are so sunken, although you're so fat otherwise. Come on now, show me your teeth, come on, open your mouth.

So Casanova, because she's probably too tired to stand up and can't in any case stand high enough to see, has to go down on his knees before his mother and open his mouth. And when she's looked inside it, she says only: Yes, that's nasty. And after a long interval during which she does her knitting: But it doesn't surprise me. Even two years ago, in Vienna, when I saw you, I thought you were having difficulties with your teeth.

You saw me in Vienna two years ago, he exclaims in utter astonishment.

Yes, and even at that time it struck me that you weren't laughing so much anymore. Instead, you'd taken to a kind of grinning, which wasn't any pleasure to see. Because people weren't supposed to see those stumps, wasn't that it? But I can't help you there, either.

Ah, Mama, he says, lack of teeth isn't the only reason for my not laughing . . .

Hardly any of the lower ones are left . . .

. . . there are other reasons, more terrible reasons why I laugh so little.

You can tell me about that later, she says and makes a dismissive gesture. When I saw you in Vienna . . .

Ah, so she saw me in Vienna, he thinks. But how, he exclaims, how is it you saw me in Vienna?

Of course, you didn't see me, she says. It was at Prince Kaunitz's. You'd been banished again, along with your little coach. And you'd wanted to hand him one of your famous appeals, in which you always describe yourself as an insect lying on its back, about to be trodden on. My word, what ideas you do have, the things you think up. But Kaunitz kept you waiting and was having dinner in the next room, and then the insect, which was supposed to be trodden on, got impatient and ran off. Do you know that I was sitting behind the Spanish screen and having dinner with him? Off silver platters, as is his custom. I'd even considered whether I shouldn't perhaps put in a good word for you, but then it just hadn't been possible, and the next day I had other worries, of course, I had to move on and I thought no more of it. Did he allow your appeal at that time?

He refused it.

So you had to move on, too?

Yes.

Well, his mother says, in any case we were very close to each other for a little while that evening, even if there was a screen between us, and though we both had to move on we breathed the same air, so to speak, and might almost have seen each other. It was the same in Turin, three years ago, we were close to each other there, as well. But you didn't see me there, either. Probably your eyes, too, aren't what they were. You should get yourself some glasses made.

I'd thought of that.

But you're too vain, isn't that it? Listen, she says, I have to be leaving soon and so far our conversation hasn't been very productive. But since chance or necessity or the general connectedness of things has after all willed it, and since we've met once again and it's not likely we'll have another meeting, you ought to answer for me a few questions which I prepared a long time ago and have been carrying around with me ever since. But naturally every mother would like to know what's become of the person she gave life to, especially if he's her only son. She'd like to know what this only son, after she's taken so much trouble with him, has actually done with his life. So tell me quickly, Giacomo, what have you done with your life?

Oh God, Casanova thinks, what sort of a question is that, what can I possibly say? And she's in a hurry as well. And she's regretting the encounter, which for him, even if he wasn't exactly delighted about it, hadn't so far been unpleasant, well, almost so. If only she'd give him a little peace, instead of always asking such questions! But it's of course quite impossible for him simply to get up and run off, considering they haven't seen each other for such a long time, even less can he simply push her out of her room, as he'd sometimes done with other women who'd asked similarly unpleasant questions. For the walk in the graveyard, but especially the conversation with the gravestone, and the encounter with the rat as well, had exhausted him much more than he'd supposed, he can feel it now. So that he can hardly think clearly and best of all he'd like to sit on the certainly very comfortable sofa beside his mother, or, even better, stretch out on it, so as to gather, in a short but deep sleep, the forces so urgently required for answering such a difficult question. But for even the shortest stretching out this sofa, even if he were to stretch his legs out full length and push his mother into a corner or off the sofa entirely, is much too short, of course. All he can do is exclaim: Oh God, what should I say?

Tell me the main thing, Giacomo, his mother says and with her free hand she traces a wide circle, I've got no time for the little things. Tell me the main thing you've done with your life, and if you're happy.

If I'm . . . , Casanova asks and he startles.

Yes, his mother says. And since he's morose and silent: So you're not happy! And what have you done with your life?

Well, Casanova says, for instance I did escape from the Piombi.

I know that, she says. And what else? And since he's silent again: So you haven't done anything with your life? So you've become the superficial and frivolous person people tell me about, something I've always feared. And to think you had such wonderful eyes, when you were a child! And what a face you had, ah God, just to think of it! If only you yourself could see the face you once had, she exclaims, you'd know what I'm talking about now. A face that was at least one in a thousand. How happy I was in those days, that my son should have that face! And what have you done with your face?

God, and what sort of a question is that, Casanova thinks, why does she keep harping on my face? As if I had no other worries! Only the face, always. What could I have done with it, considering the way of the world? And naturally faces grow older too. But don't you understand, Mama, he exclaims, after I escaped from the Piombi I was always on the run.

On the run, his mother exclaims. We're all on the run. That's no excuse.

56

But I was quite particularly on the run, he says. Just think: Since then, I've hardly left my coach. Perhaps you think that was a comfortable situation? Yet it seems that nobody, no country, no city, wants me.

There'll be reasons for that.

And with people too, he says, look, I don't know if it's my fault, but with people I have only very fugitive relationships.

You mean with women, she says.

With people, he says.

And why do you have so many women?

From despair.

At what?

At myself.

And how can you despair at yourself with the face that I gave you, she says. So it's true, what I've heard about you. Shame on you! No wonder they always come to me afterward, to complain and have a good cry. And then I never know what to tell the poor creatures, when you've abandoned or betrayed them.

They come to you?

Who else? she exclaims. They open their hearts to me, it's me they tell what you do with them.

Mama, Casanova exclaims, all I do is have them help me to stand up straight.

You humiliate them.

But I get humiliated too.

They come all scratches and tatters.

I get my claws into them.

And those bites!

Out of despair, Mama!

And then I can't sleep. While you dedicate your
nights to your lusts, I lie in my bed and tell myself:
So that's what's become of him—a pig!

Mama!

Yes indeed, a pig.

But Mama, I'm also a poet.

What?

At least, I live poetically, Casanova exclaims and at
once he regrets having said it, because his mother
probably won't believe him. Also the explanation
he owes his mother is such a difficult one that in
earlier times she'd have understood it, if at all, only
with the greatest effort, while now, the way he knows
her to be, she probably won't understand it in the
slightest. And besides, the brains behind the once-
so-handsome face are especially sluggish today.
Nevertheless, he'll explain the matter to her, particularly since he hopes that, once he's done so, he'll
arrive at a better understanding of himself and of
the other thing. Look, he therefore says, and in the
narrow chair where he's sitting he spreads his arms.
And he tries to show her that in his case it's a big
mistake to suppose that comedies were what he had
to write.

You and comedies, she interrupts him at once, don't make me laugh.

... Or memoirs, if you like.

To double your pleasures, she exclaims. I tell you, you're a pig.

Well, it's a mistake to suppose that he, Casanova, had to write or compose something, or, like Monsieur Voltaire, put it on the stage, in order to be a poet. For him, he exclaims, that may be necessary, but not for me. For him (Casanova) to be a poet, it had so far always been enough to feel at every moment the complete unreality of his existence. He had always been, figuratively of course, the work of art himself, but she probably wouldn't understand this. So that people shouldn't believe a word he says in the way an opinion is usually believed, that is, as an expression of a nature that's identical with itself. He, as a living work of art (not as actor!), which is how he's always felt himself to be, as other people have, didn't possess a nature that was identical with itself. Instead of pouring his imagination out on paper, he'd taken it into life with him, carried it out in life. Also the women he'd loved, with a passion completely authentic, whether his mother believed it or not, he'd invented them all. And even the confusions, even the most desperate ones, in which he'd been involved again and again, these too, he'd willed them and thought them up out of the depths of his artistic imagination. His mother might believe there was a gulf between art and life, but until recently, as far as he was concerned, there'd been no such gulf, he'd overcome it, canceled it, closed it, insofar as he'd been art himself, right down to the pleats in his clothing and the clearing of his throat. So that everything he did or had done, at least until recently, had been poetic. But suddenly, he didn't know why as yet, *something else* had very ruthlessly thrust itself into the foreground, so that, try as he might, the poetic thing was getting to be harder and harder for him to achieve. And nowadays it seemed that soon there'd be no poetry left, and that the art would pass away from him, even before life itself did.

Yet his mother, as he'd foreseen, naturally doesn't understand all this. Yes, she exclaims from her corner, and I can't sleep, whereas every night of yours is spent on your little artistic tricks . . .

My nights? How do you know what I'm . . .

What you're doing? Just go to the window and take a look.

And Casanova, after extricating himself with great effort from his armchair, which grips him like a vise, goes to the window. Look, he thinks, that's the backyard of the Steadfast Saint, where you got down from your coach. Look, and there's your coach! And how close to her window the coach is, although her window is so high up.

Right, his mother says, that's the backyard where you've had your coach parked for three whole days, probably to save money on a room, directly beneath my window. And every time I go to the window for a breath of air, my gaze falls right on it, right on the *coach bed* with its famous artistic mechanism, which people have naturally told me about. And into which you lured last night the Pocchini girl, with whom you quite shamelessly ...

But Mama, Casanova exclaims—he doesn't want to be reminded of last night—she never came.

Don't tell me lies! With my own eyes I saw her crawling into your vehicle.

But Mama, it was morning by the time she came, Casanova exclaims, relieved because now at last his mother is in the wrong. For he can remember quite clearly how he'd had to pester the girl, practically all night, first beside the pigsty and then behind the barn, until toward daybreak, before crawling into her hayloft, she'd crawled for a minute into his coach.

And whose services, night or morning, it's all the same, his mother mercilessly continues, you did then pay for, probably far too well. And I had to look on and see everything you were doing with her, you animal!

But Mama, Casanova exclaims and he's sweating more profusely than ever, his hands, his forehead, but of course especially his armpits. Yes, it's really high time to give a thought to his sponges. Which, under his mother's questioning and during her answers too, have become saturated, so that he hasn't been able for quite a time to accompany his remarks with the usual elegant and expressive gestures. Yes,

sheer fright that the collected fluids might spurt
out under his mother's very eyes almost prevents
him from moving his arms. And how can he talk,
how can he justify himself, if he mayn't move his
arms? Wring the sponges out, he thinks, wring them
out at once. But where should he wring them out?
Her room is so small, everything in clear sight, out
of the question to do it there. And the window?
Couldn't one inconspicuously extract the sponges
from one's sleeves, hold them outside, wring them
out of the window? Ridiculous, the very idea of
extracting something inconspicuously in his mother's presence and holding it out of the window. No,
he thinks, you'll have to wait until she takes a nap,
surely she'll feel tired sometime and fall asleep?
And then with plenty of water you'll clean the room,
quickly and thoroughly (especially beneath the sofa
and the bed, those areas he'll thoroughly clean), and
after cleaning you'll slip out of her room for a moment, and then downstairs, perhaps behind the hotel, perhaps between the hotel and the stables . . .
Yet who's to say if his mother will really sleep, she
doesn't look at all tired. Not once yet has she yawned,
whereas he hasn't been able to stop yawning ever
since he came into the room. Also he can't help
thinking of all the stairs he'd have to climb up again,
if ever he could succeed in wringing the sponges
out and shaking them dry, surely climbing back up
the stairs would make him sweat all over again, so
nothing much would be gained by a single rapid
wringing out and shaking dry behind the stables.
And altogether: How can he leave the room with a

mother like this, who never thinks of taking a nap, but keeps on badgering him with her nasty reproaches and difficult questions.

No, Mama, he exclaims, you're mistaken, she gave me nothing at all, she only laughed at me. For a long time now, as soon as I make advances, women have been avoiding . . .

Don't tell lies, his mother exclaims. Only last May you deflowered Signorina Lepi.

But nobody else wanted her, he exclaims, she's a humpback. Neither she nor I had any illusions.

You sweated through seven shirts with her.

But how . . .

And I was always so proud of you, his mother says. And what have I got to be proud of now? You were such a tall and handsome son, and what's become of you?

Forgive me, Mother, forgive me, Casanova exclaims, but sometimes I'm so sad, so desperate. And then I want to distract myself, strengthen myself. They've banished me now—something you won't know—from Bologna too.

Why?

Debts.

Just like it was in Turin three years ago, because of debts you were banished from there, too. But before that, in the theater, in that box: Shame on you, you had two women at once, Signorina Borgello and Signorina Alfani.

Ah, yes, he says, I remember, you too were in Turin.

Of course I was in Turin, his mother exclaims and angrily she stamps her small feet. Yes, you can look amazed. Imagine how amazed *I* was. I couldn't believe my eyes when I saw you, at your age, with so many young women suddenly in your box. Actually I should have spoken to you there and then, but after everything I'd seen I had no inclination to.

But how can you have seen?

What a question, his mother exclaims. I was up there on the stage, where you can see everything. I could see from the stage directly into your box.

But the box, exclaims Casanova who actually blushes a little at the thought that his mother could have seen everything he's done in his life, or even most things, the box, he says, is much higher than the stage.

Exactly, his mother exclaims.

And anyway, he exclaims, what were you doing up on the stage in Turin? Have you become an actress?

Nowadays I only figure as an extra, his mother says, but earlier I was an actress. Once I was even a dancer. Here, she exclaims, because you probably don't believe me. And she stoops and quickly and artfully raises her black skirt, under which many other skirts are hiding, white ones too, even red ones and green ones, raises it far too high, right up above her knees, so that he can see her legs, which are skinny, but, for such an old woman, still appreciable and shapely. On them, as he then sees, the black

silk stockings are all twisted and hanging slackly
down in lumps. God, he thinks, why is she showing
me this? For it was the last thing a man in his state
wants to see. God, he thinks, what if one always
knew what's hanging from mothers' legs inside,
however dapper they may look on the outside? And
his mother doesn't make any attempt to pull her
stockings up again, she just lets them hang. She
wants to show you how badly you've neglected her,
Casanova thinks, and he's on the verge of stooping
to remove at least this reproach from the world,
and, even if he doesn't clean the room for her, to
pull his mother's stockings up, but then suddenly
he's horrified by her skinny legs, even more so than
by her thick hair, so he doesn't stoop after all, but
leaves everything hanging and simply looks away
from the lumps. And so when I couldn't kick these
legs up high enough anymore, his mother continues, when she's sure he's not for the present going
to pull her stockings up and pinch the lumps out,
here, at least take a look at them, she exclaims and
begins, so that she'll have his attention, to kick her
skinny legs about a bit, well, then I became a singer,
out of sheer desperation. And so you'll believe that
too and won't believe I'm poetically inventing anything, she exclaims and spreads her arms. My God,
thinks Casanova who still hasn't got over the terrible disorder under her skirt, whatever is she going
to show me next? Shouldn't she be a bit more sedate
at her age? But then she throws back her head, shuts
her eyes, and utters, before he can stop her, with
her mouth wide open, several notes, which for such

an old and wrinkled woman are indeed astonishingly rich and beautiful. She can really sing, too,
thinks Casanova, who feels awkward, of course, to
be hearing his old mother, in the dark and tiny
room, suddenly and for no reason singing at the top
of her voice, especially since she opens her mouth
so wide that without wanting to do so he has to
look deep into her throat. So he knows what his
mother has got not only under her skirt but also in
her throat.

Well? she asks when she's finished.

Yet Casanova declines to comment on the song.

But couldn't you hear from my voice how good it
used to be, she asks.

Let's not speak of it, Mama, he says.

And why won't you admit that I sing well? Can you
do it any better, perhaps? she asks.

What does she want of me, Casanova thinks, why
is she so insistent? Am I supposed to sing too, perhaps? And because hitherto he's considered himself
a tolerable singer, who has counted many real sing-
ers among his mistresses and has passed many hours,
though backstage, *singing* with them, he's making
ready to open his own mouth and sing to his mother,
spreading his arms in the appropriate manner, an
old coachman's song he once heard in Sardinia and
always enjoyed singing, but then he tells himself
that, considering the agitated mood she's in, he certainly wouldn't be able to rival her, however wide
he might open his mouth to sing his song. So he

retracts his already outspread arms and lays them in his lap. I don't have to be able to sing, he says, I'm a poet, not a castrato.

And I was a respected singer, his mother exclaims, how can you make any comparison? And once again she opens her crone's mouth to let out a few more trills left over from the time before. You hear? she exclaims, that's how I sing nowadays. That'll give you an idea of how I must have sung once upon a time. Then unfortunately my voice weakened. Probably because of my being troubled about you.

And what did you . . . perform that evening in Turin, Casanova asks—they've talked about singing far too long already, for his taste.

Naturally I was the wife of the rich miser Pozzi, his mother says.

Ah yes, I remember now, says Casanova, who naturally doesn't remember, you were wearing a blue dress.

No, his mother exclaims, I was wearing a green one. And then she even stamps her feet because he hadn't noticed the color of her dress. But that doesn't surprise me, she adds, in your box you were probably too occupied with the wardrobe of your ladies to notice your old mother, who on that evening walked right to the front of the stage and acted, as we actors say, the soul out of her body, all for you alone. And all the time I was looking up at your box and blowing you kisses, although that's strictly forbidden. And you, she exclaims, you didn't even notice me!

But of course I noticed you, I remember now, quite precisely, Casanova says though he's completely forgotten her performance at that time, as well as the whole play in which she claims she acted. How awkward that he should have paid so little attention to events on the stage on that occasion, but how could he have known that she was suddenly standing up there, when actually she was dead? Awkward, too, that his coach is standing directly under the window. Why on earth did the coachman follow him here, instead of waiting at the watering place? And through the small coach window, across which, awkward too, not even the curtain is drawn, Casanova's gaze falls again on the coach bed, actually still rumpled from the morning. No wonder his mother, who's already suspicious enough, thinks at once the very worst when she sees the deeply rumpled bed. Yet he remembers quite precisely that nothing that could dismay her had happened last night in this anyway so terribly uncomfortable bed. After a long parley and for a high price (practically the last of his money) he'd been able to persuade the Pocchini girl at daybreak (it had taken that long beside the pigsty to talk her into it) to crawl with him into the coach, but only, as he had assured her, because he needed something warm on his left side, where for months past, as soon as he'd lie down, he'd been feeling a dull and quite artless ache. Which, or so he'd convinced himself, a naked young body always mitigated somewhat. And he hadn't wanted anything more from this young person: only that she should press firmly up against his left side and drive the pain away by keeping still. That his need to have her warmth as close as possible to his pain had finally made him toss and turn and rumple the bedclothes, that was something his mother couldn't blame him for. Unless the disarrangement of the bed had happened only after the Pocchini girl's departure, when, long into the morning, probably half-unconsciously, he'd groped and reached for her everywhere in the empty coach bed, of course in vain, because she'd long since gone back to her hayloft, back to the animals. But of his mother's ever believing this there was no prospect whatever. The best thing would be to draw the curtain and think no more of it.

You know, Mama, he says when he's drawn the curtain again and walked away from the window, I can remember quite clearly now your performance in Turin, but to tell you the truth you're rather a middling actress. Now that by chance we've seen each other again and there can be no question of further performances, I can tell you this. For I wouldn't allow you to go on the stage again. Least of all as an extra.

Whether I'm a good or bad actress is not for you to judge, his mother says from her sofa and she gently strokes her skirt, in order to compound his confusion about what is under it. Perhaps, she says, you do understand something about women (I doubt it), but about art, even if you're constantly talking about it, you obviously don't understand a thing. Otherwise you'd know it was a thoroughly respectable role I was playing then. Perhaps the most respectable role in the whole play, if not in every play that exists. I refused all six propositions that were made to me in five acts, and thus I forewent a lot of money. And now hold my wool, she exclaims and throws him her black ball of wool.

Mama, says Casanova and catches the ball and forces himself back into his chair, I don't want to see you going onto the stage. I don't want you to be seen on the stage still, even in a so-called *respectable* role. What sort of a company is it?

What sort of a company? his mother exclaims. An old and honorable Italian traveling company, of course, which plays only in the best theaters.

An Italian traveling company, Casanova exclaims in dismay, but they're the worst of all! They're notorious all over Europe for their wicked morals.

Nonsense, his mother interrupts him, people exaggerate a lot, especially people like you. But I see that one can't talk about art with you, because you have prejudices. Well, perhaps at least you've got clever hands and can help me with something practical. Perhaps you can close my trunk. Over there, by the wall.

And Casanova, who doesn't know which of her two commissions comes first, holding the wool or closing the trunk (for in his state he can't execute both at the same time), decides that first he'll hold the wool for a while and then lay it down in his armchair and quickly stand up to close the trunk, which

he'd entirely overlooked till now. From his armchair, nonetheless, he now looks more closely at this
trunk, which is standing under the window. The lid
is open, a moderately high, moderately wide trunk,
but a very long one, probably made of heavy wood
and then painted black, a trunk for long journeys
overseas, with room for many things and a great
variety of things, he sees it, with carved ornaments
at its ends, the kind one doesn't often see anymore.
There are also two bronze handles by which to carry
it. And how should his frail mother carry the heavy
trunk? Curious that such a small woman should
travel with such a big trunk. And since he's now
become curious and would like to know what she
has packed into her trunk, but can't see it all from
his armchair, he asks: What's in it?

That's none of your business, his mother says and
makes with her knitting hands a few impatient gestures, with which, though earlier she'd drawn his
attention to the trunk, she now probably intends to
distract his attention.

If you don't want to tell me, I'll have a look for
myself, Casanova says. And before his mother—who,
to be sure, can still sing loudly and knit quickly (the
black shirt emerging from her hands is now assum-
ing distinct shapes, look, there's a second arm growing out of her lap!), but can only with great effort
raise herself up from such a low sofa—can restrain
him, he has laid the wool aside and is already standing by the trunk. Which is full to the brim with fine
lace garments and panties and bonnets and fabrics,

all black, all black! Lace, Casanova exclaims. These fine and expensive lace things, what do you need them for, at your age?

We're neither of us young anymore, his mother says.

Mama, says Casanova, who's standing at the window once again, without knowing why, I want an answer now. Why at your age do you still need these lace things?

Oh you, with all your questions, his mother says— evidently she's embarrassed by the question. What do I need them for? I've taken a few young actresses under my wing, I teach them their craft. True, it's a strain and it only earns me a few cents, but one has to earn a living somehow. Ah, she exclaims, what do you know about it, you're a man and supposedly an artist as well, who doesn't have much to do with reality. But the life of a woman who's simply too old now to be an artist is quite different from what you men imagine. Our life is so, so . . . But then she doesn't tell him what the lives of older women are like, but only gives him an example. For example, she says, being constantly on the move is simply unbearable for a woman of my age. Arriving, unpacking, going into a strange room, but you've hardly gone into the room and unpacked when you have to pack up again and leave! And the coaches, how they bump! The mere sight of a coach makes me feel quite sick nowadays. But who's interested in it all now? Who in all the world thinks about an old woman like that?

I do, Casanova exclaims in a loud voice and he walks, so as not to be looking anymore at his rumpled coach bed, to his mother on the sofa. And he's meaning to rest a hand on her shoulder, as a sign of his support, but, on account of the knitting needles in her hands, he thinks better of it. Instead, he exclaims once more: I do! and he stands up as tall as he can in the low room. So that, if he too hadn't shrunk somewhat during the last few years, he might certainly have hit the ceiling with the interesting head he'd so artfully laid in the laps of so many women. I do, he exclaims for a third time. For, he then adds, I am your son. Therefore, from now on, I'll look after you.

You, she exclaims and she starts to laugh. But what laughter. He, in any case, can't hear it. Mama, he exclaims, stop it now. To think, he says, that my mother has to travel so much, and with a theater company too! (He means that he can't endure the thought.) And what's more, with an Italian traveling company, he exclaims. I know what goes on in the dressing rooms of extras, after the play, and between the acts.

Not with us, his mother exclaims, we're a clean company.

In the whole world there's not one clean company, Casanova exclaims, and I forbid it.

Then his mother sits up straight as an arrow, so to speak (as straight as a woman of her age can sit up) and exclaims: You greenhorn, who are you, to forbid me anything? And to punish him as quickly as she can: Give me my wool back! Do you know what it's like to be a woman who's getting older? And older. And still older. Do you know how one clings to every shred of hope in those long nights? And what thoughts come to one's mind? And her four husbands are long buried and her only son is like him, not caring for her, but going down in history perhaps as the biggest pig in Europe?

Mama, Casanova exclaims.

Look at this room you let me live in, his mother exclaims and she spreads her arms again, as if at any moment she might fly or at least sing again. Look at this low ceiling. Couldn't you have told them to make it a bit higher? And the sofa I have to sit on, she exclaims, couldn't you at least have had them install a better sofa? Perhaps you think it's a soft and comfortable sofa, because you're always standing at the window, and from the window the sofa might look soft and comfortable, but that's where you're mistaken. If you don't believe me, sit down beside me, then you'll know.

No, says Casanova, who can't bear the thought of sitting beside his mother on such a small sofa.

You see, she says, and yet you leave me sitting here. Admit now that it's outrageous. Yes, you've done nothing but outrage me. This filth, she continues, my God, this filth! And not only in this room, but wherever my feet carry me: this filth, filth, filth! On the furniture, the walls, yes, even in the bed! Your poor old mother has hardly blown the candle out and closed her eyes when she thinks of the filth you've made her lie down in again. And you've left me stranded in this filth, she exclaims, for thirty-three years. Ah, Giacomo, why are you like that? And it seems she's really going to burst into tears over her hard-hearted son, but he turns his back on her.

I wouldn't have thought, he says, that my mother could go on the stage as an extra. You ought to be ashamed, Mama! Really now!

Then his mother lays aside her knitting needles and stands laboriously up and falls laboriously on her knees, and she embraces, just as she learned to do on the stage, thus with great fervor, his long bony legs, and she exclaims: Forgive me!

Never, he exclaims.

And his mother, wanting for some reason known only to her to continue the embarrassing scene, exclaims: Then kiss me good-bye, at least! And when he doesn't kiss her either: At least on the cheek, she exclaims. And after she's got to her feet she raises her cheek, with its strange dark blotches, for him to kiss. And when he doesn't kiss her cheek either, she asks: May I at least kiss you?

No, Casanova says.

Then she sits down on the sofa again. And where are you going now, she asks.

He says he's on his way to Naples, with a letter of introduction from Count Scarpi in his pocket. For Scarpi had connections with . . .

And me, his mother says, in three days I have an engagement in Cremona. For now they were going to the smaller towns, the company wasn't big enough for the big ones. But she could lend him a taler, if he . . .

Casanova: Thank you. Perhaps I can . . .

His mother: Thank you. Is the coach yours?

No, Casanova lies. Because the thought of sharing the black upholstery with his little mother, possibly at night too, and possibly at speed on a bumpy road that would fling everything about and his mother, light as a bird, against his chest . . . No, Casanova thinks and he walks to the door.

Otherwise, his mother says, we might have traveled a bit of the way together. Well, she says, next time perhaps. Good-bye, Giacomo!

Adieu, Mama!

13

And then, after he's left his mother to her low room, which he hasn't even cleaned, left her without hesitation, the sponges now freshly wrung out, solitary in his crate of a coach, burrowed deep into the black upholstery—his road goes along a slope and on the cheek of this slope . . .

Where to? the coachman shouts.

Straight ahead.

Then, without telling him to stop, Casanova writes
a few sentences in his memoirs, which he's begun
to write, because personally he has no more illusions. (Amongst other things he'd like to prove that
he has lived.) Thus: a few sentences, which he immediately crosses out, because they're too gloomy.
He prefers to present himself as he was at the beginning, serene, superficial. For example he writes:
Behind my effort to return to my homeland there
lies naturally the wish to return to my origins, and
the blessing I crave would be to *start afresh* . . .
Repetition, therefore, as a movement to reverse
memory. A longing to remember continuously, but
into the future. Yet he crosses this out, too.

Or he writes this and immediately crosses it out:
During this remarkable encounter which I want now
quickly to forget, not only did my mother not speak
to me about my worries, also the essence for my
hair, which she'd promised me and which, even if
it hadn't helped me, wouldn't have harmed me . . .

Or he writes this and crosses it out: The region we're
now entering in our coach is a wide and rocky ter-
rain without inhabitants, over which black birds
(jackdaws?) fly croaking in their circles. So that
when the coachman asks once more which direction
he's to take, but we've already taken all possible
directions and come to nothing, we climb out and
look for one last time also in directions that are
possible for a while among the possible abysses and
ravines, walk along the edges of them, he writes,
only then to sink down dejected on the debris of

which that world consists, until from black clouds above us . . . black drops upon us . . . Clearly, he writes, the gist of the whole thing is to make endurable, with a modicum of art, a way downward, at the end of which stands, with no art at all, death.

Tolstoy's Head

Not many people know that after the Russian Revolution Leo Leovich Tolstoy, son of the writer Leo Nikolayevich Tolstoy, went to America to portray for American audiences, in circus acts and films, his father, whom he detested, and to whom he bore an outward resemblance so striking that it often made things difficult, because his head was much smaller than his father's had been.

It was the fate of any refugee—Tolstoy Junior was making his getaway, doing so, as he himself put it, to avoid being "hanged by my own serfs from one of the birch trees the old man had planted in Yasnaya Polyana, those very serfs he'd always been chattering about." Leo Leovich has opted for the "radical solution," and, while crossing the Atlantic on board the steamer *Democracy*, he meets up with the impresario J. W. Katz from Lublin. And it is Katz, a plump young Pole, who, during a stroll on the deck, after observing Tolstoy at length and from every angle, has the idea of persuading him to make public appearances in America, impersonating his own father, for money.

At first Leo Leovich doesn't understand him. Like his father when young, he feels he's an artist, but he's boring as a writer, as a sculptor he's bad, and, as can be imagined, he's very envious of his world-famous progenitor, impersonating whom is one of the few things he hasn't yet had a shot at. Day after day now he leans with Katz against the railing and they discuss what might be done. After their arrival, with the Goddess of Liberty in sight, they shake hands on their project, thirty percent of which, excluding fees, will go to J. W. Katz. Then with the remnant of their money they travel by railroad together across the continent, through the unbelievable heat, to Los Angeles, where, on July 30, they take a noisy attic room in a hotel owned by a cutthroat Italian—Casa Mia. The room, empty except for two metal bedsteads, is the cheapest in the cheap hotel. After two or three sleepless nights in this barn of a building—until recently it was a barn, but at the moment it's the only hotel in the vicinity of the studios—Katz manages to introduce his protégé to the director-producer L. A. Goodman. Tolstoy Junior, following Katz's advice, has slipped for this encounter into his father's attire, the long smock, the velour trousers, and the tall knee boots, which he always carries around with him in one of his two suitcases, and which, now that the revolution has put a stop to quarrels regarding the family estate, are his only patrimony. Immediately he makes upon Goodman (also a Pole) the impression Katz has foreseen. Goodman looks at him, takes a step back, and is obliged, hand clutching forehead, to prop himself against a wall. In younger days a distant devotee of the older Tolstoy's works and vision of the world, even obsessively so, he can't believe his eyes, he's flabbergasted. True, he never actually saw the old man, but he knows him from many photographs, so that, even in the darkness of this first evening, he finds the resemblance perfect, and at once he accepts Katz's proposition to cast Tolstoy Junior in a film about Tolstoy Senior, dead now for exactly ten years. Feeling so close to greatness he keeps trying to lay his hand on Tolstoy Junior's shoulder, but the latter, disliking both Poles, pushes it away. But when Goodman sits at lunch next day, together with Fred Seller, his makeup man, face to face with Tolstoy Junior—Goodman has no style, all he's ordered is sandwiches and Coca-Cola—he's surprised by what he sees in the daylight. Tell him, he says to Katz who's interpreting for Tolstoy, that in my opinion there can be no question of his portraying his father as a young man, he's much too old for that. A pity, of course it takes some of the attraction out of our project. I don't know what he's been doing, but yesterday I thought he was younger, he adds reproachfully. Younger, well now, says J. W. Katz, and he looks at Tolstoy Junior, who is

getting on for sixty at this time. And who, like most
sons, doesn't like always to be compared with his
father, hence his utmost reluctance to consent to
portray him. Meanwhile Katz has furtively pushed
Tolstoy's head, which is oldish and decrepit, sure
enough, into the shadow and is blaming its condition on troubles with money, bad health, the strains
of being a refugee, repeated failures in his career
as an artist, and family relationships—Tolstoy Junior has been divorced several times and has children, living or dead, all over the world—as well as
the revolution. For all that, J. W. Katz says, he is
his father. All the same, says L. A. Goodman, he was
younger yesterday. And he sits there in an oppres-
sive silence for a while, and then advises Tolstoy
Junior, even though he really won't be able to use
him now as "the young Tolstoy," at least to stand
up straight and, since he certainly is just like his
father, tall, slim, despotic, and proud of his name
and title, to "talk down" to people. Good, Katz says,
we'll include that in the contract. Meanwhile Mr.
Seller, who during the conversation has been si-
lently comparing Tolstoy Junior with a photograph
of the older Tolstoy, which Katz has pressed into
his hands as proof of the resemblance, raises an
even more serious question. He has noticed that
despite the amazing resemblance Tolstoy Junior's
head is much smaller than the old man's, in fact it
is ridiculously small. With a head as small as that,
he says, we'll never make on the American public
the desired impression, which has to rest on an
altogether natural and immediately striking resem-

blance. But, Katz exclaims, he really is Tolstoy's son! and he shouts to Tolstoy Junior: Tell him, Leo! And the latter, Katz having rehearsed him in the proper English words, stands up, knocks on his chest, and proclaims, down to his hosts at the table below: I am the son, Mr. Seller, I am the son! And true enough, Mr. Goodman that very day signs a contract of engagement for ten weeks, at two hundred and fifty dollars a week, lays an advance of one hundred dollars cash on the table, and, after Mr. Seller has promised to fix the head, they go about their sundry concerns, each in his own direction, through the heat of the day.

Since work on the film won't begin for two days, Tolstoy and Katz have a chance to look around the studio and familiarize themselves with what goes on in front of the camera, also behind it. This studio, to which they travel by streetcar, is surrounded by a tall green fence. Inquisitive people cling to the fence, as if stuck there, and peer through the gaps in it, even when no filming is in progress. As soon as they show L. A. Goodman's card, J. W. Katz and Tolstoy Junior are admitted, allowed to walk right in and, just so long as they don't get in front of a camera that's rolling and so into the wrong film (three are being made at the same time), to stroll as they please up and down the various streets, which are nothing but facades, to tap on the walls of houses, and look into the windows that can't be seen through. Since new scenes are constantly needed, the facades are ceaselessly being torn down by the carpenters and set up again in some other

shape, without anyone quite knowing what it's all
about. The doors and windows too, through which
the actors have to walk or jump, are constantly
being set up somewhere else, often for the sheer fun
of it, gateways and chimneys are set up together
with them, or else carted away again. During the
noon hour they watch as the actors—because there's
a break for lunch—dash across a freshly paved artificial street in their contradictory costumes, in
order to buy, in a small but real shop, bread and
soft American cheese. From above there falls, into
the studio where Tolstoy Junior will soon be his
own deceased father, the light for working by. This
light is unnatural and uniformly white, and it is
produced in the following way: Bedsheets sewn together and hung from cords are stretched between
long poles and hoisted up into the Californian sky.
Thus the sunlight falls through them, and by them
it is softened. With his feet wide apart, leaning heavily
on his stick, and, apart from his head, just like his
father when the latter could still gaze into the sun-
shine, Tolstoy Junior stands facing up into the sheets
and blinking into the light. J. W. Katz, meanwhile,
with his hands clasped behind him, strides back
and forth under the sheets and is already musing
about an extension of the contract, with his share
increased to thirty-five percent. Thus they look on
while, as cameras roll, workers who are emigrants
like themselves transport the sheets, following the
sun's path, like giant flags through the studio. At
evening, when the sun has sunk below the green
fence, the sheets are folded up and stored away for
the night.

Tolstoy's Head

The administration building of the company
employing Tolstoy Junior was originally a farm-
house. On the ground floor, which still smells of
the cow barn that was once next door—you can
smell cow barn—he is shown into his dressing room,
one that he will be sharing with two other performers. Into this longish room, partitioned by screens,
with a hanging triptych mirror and crammed with
numerous pots of lotion and makeup, marches on
the next morning Mr. Seller, who has meanwhile
had the photographs of the old Tolstoy enlarged.
He has come to fix the head, no doubt about that.
Tolstoy Junior has to seat himself in his dressing-
room chair, so that Seller, photographs of the old
man in hand, can tiptoe around him and feel his
head, something repugnant to the younger Tolstoy.
Tell him to stop it, he keeps saying in Russian to
J. W. Katz, but there's not much Katz can do. Finally Mr. Seller extracts from the linen bag he carries with him an assortment of tufts and hanks of
hair, muslin strips and wads of cotton waste, which
he fastens artfully and affectionately to Tolstoy's
little head. The latter is of course unaccustomed to
such attentions, to having his head inflated like this.
Hands and feet stretched far out he lies sprawled
in his folding chair and wipes with a towel—it's
August now—the sweat from his face. Just keep still,
Mr. Seller says. And explains to him that he's making out of the materials he's brought a wig beneath
which he will stuff gauze, muslin, and netting, so
as to enlarge the head. To indicate his aging—should
that play any part in the film—he will make several
versions of this wig, enough to show distinctly the

successive stages of decay affecting hair and head as he gets older.

Between you and me, J. W. Katz asks, is his head really so small?

Yes, says Mr. Seller and he goes on gluing.

At this point word has traveled around the studio as to who is there. Actors and extras keep surging into Tolstoy's room; some show their cards, which they leave on the dressing table. Many of these till now—one can tell from the way they walk—have been acting cowboy parts, but for the duration of Tolstoy's film the film company has fitted them out in Russian costumes. They crowd around his chair, because, not knowing why, they want to touch him, at least once, before the filming is over. Secretaries and cashiers come too, people who earn only twelve dollars a week and want to draw him into a conversation about the advantages of America, though they fail to do so.

Next morning, when the sun is in the sky behind the bedsheets again and Tolstoy Junior's new head is complete, L. A. Goodman takes Tolstoy and Katz aside. And explains to them that although he's read a few books by Tolstoy's father, at least the most important ones—he's no intellectual—the film has no screenplay. We have no advance plan, he says, the ideas will come up as we work, and when an idea does come up, we'll go after it. From him too, he says to Katz, pointing at Tolstoy, we're hoping for some inspiration, which we'll develop, once we've begun filming. Translate that for him, Johann, he says to Katz. Tolstoy Junior, who, like all less gifted people, would naturally have preferred to work from a finished screenplay, with actions and positions and pauses all prescribed, and who'd altogether have liked to know in detail what was expected of him regarding his portrayal of his father, shrugs his shoulders. And wonders how his father would have behaved in such a situation, portraying himself in front of a camera, although he'd been spared any such thing. Well, in any case I'm his son, he thinks when he espies the big supporting cast, people who, as former circus people or boxers, have probably never heard of his father and are now attired as "Tolstoyans," Russian country folk, or even as close relatives (actually long dead)—they're all peeking in at him through the low-set window of his dressing room.

And now with J. W. Katz's help he ventures at least a description of the paternal house, where supposedly his father was born on a leather sofa on the veranda and where he spent part of his childhood. Unfortunately many of the expressions he uses have no equivalents in American, so they can't be translated, or else Katz the Pole who is translating doesn't understand the Russian words, or else Tolstoy Junior has simply forgotten important features of the house along with the words for them, because, since that time, he has seen so much else—all of it unbelievable—and therefore he's unable to describe them. For example, he's not at all sure of himself when describing the sunny upper floor which his father had all to himself and where large parts of the film are supposed to be

set. It's thus impossible for him to tell the carpenters, all of whom are clever artisans, how the
curtain-rod mechanism used to work on this floor.
These curtains were attached to the rods by thongs
of silk that Tolstoy Senior's mother used to refur-
bish throughout the year; to open or close a curtain
one had to slide the thongs very gently along the
rod. But here and now curtains hang by rough
wooden rings, so they have to be tugged roughly
and firmly along the rod. How can Tolstoy Junior
explain such subtle differences to this Katz fellow,
who often doesn't understand the simplest words
or mixes them up with something in Polish? Was
it like this? Goodman asks him when the carpenters
have finished once more the construction that is
supposed to represent the sunlit paternal upper floor.
In reply Tolstoy Junior has Katz translate: No, it
was different. Then it was probably like this? Mr.
Goodman asks, standing baffled in the wood shav-
ings when the carpenters have set up a new, totally
different sunny floor. No, Tolstoy Junior has Katz
translate, it wasn't like that, either. Again and again
the carpenters try to copy the mansion with the
shining floor upstairs, but again and again Tolstoy
Junior shakes his head. For heaven's sake, how was
it then? Goodman shouts—now that the sun sheets
are being rolled up again for the night. Different,
says Tolstoy Junior.

On Wednesday, the mansion having been constructed afresh and Tolstoy Junior, equipped for his
first scene with an enlarged head, having come to
terms with it—that was just about the way it used

to be—they have no "story." But they have to have one. A story! Goodman shouts again and again, running up and down outside the mansion with his megaphone, through which he's eager to be giving instructions to his actors. Tolstoy Junior has sat himself down in an obscure corner of the paternal upper floor and is attempting to drink Russian tea from an American paper cup, while J. W. Katz, pouring the sugar in for him, gazes down at Goodman. Then it occurs to Tolstoy Junior, while drinking his tea, that he once tried to refute his father and to poke fun at him, by writing, when he was young, a parody of "The Kreutzer Sonata," in which there's a wife whom the husband wants to dispose of, but who stays alive—a doll is buried instead of her. Perhaps he could sell this novella to Goodman? And what happens to the wife later on? Goodman shouts up to Katz. But Goodman shakes his head when he hears further remarkable features of the novella shouted by Katz over the heads of the extras. He doesn't like the story, he'd like to show his public a true-to-life, everyday episode involving the old Tolstoy. For example, how he receives, while having coffee one morning, a letter full of lies from the tsar, tosses it away, sits down at his desk, and dictates an important work to his servant. But my father never received any letters from the tsar, Tolstoy Junior has Katz translate. No matter, Goodman replies, the thing is that he could have done. So with his new head Tolstoy Junior in boots and linen smock is placed on the balcony, and from there, in the dull light, thus past the bedsheets reaching skyward, he sees the tsar's messenger approaching on horseback. He recognizes the letter in his hand, for he has quickly grasped the elements of film art: Anybody who leaves the scene to the left has to reenter it from the right. Seeing the letter he leaps up and, in the posture of his father, who suffered so much from his son's being a nonentity, strides back and forth on the sunlit floor in front of the camera. And he remembers how he himself once strode back and forth like this on another sunlit floor, when a letter from his father came to him, a letter which, supposedly because he hadn't done what his father told him to do, and because he supposedly didn't understand his father, excluded him from his father's will. And now Tolstoy Junior has in his hand again this letter that his father once wrote him. He tears it open, reads it, shakes his stuffed head. Then—all according to L. A. Goodman's directions—he lays the letter on top of the envelope and waits for the pianola to start playing. And true enough his mother and wife, Countess Sofia Tolstoy, acted by a rapidly aged Croatian circus equestrienne who has been sitting at the keyboard for a long time, begins to play, demonstrating that, by and large, she is content with all that's happening. She's happy that her son too will now become an artist, and that he'll be able to perpetuate the artistic conversations in the house, in the event of its present master ceasing to be. Now to the rhythm of her performance the young Tolstoy tears the tsar's letter to shreds and tosses them, following directions that issue from Mr. Goodman's megaphone, into the wastepaper basket. Then he settles at his desk to dictate something to his servant, and exclaims over and over again, exactly as his father had done: Cross it out! Cross it out!

Later the streets are paved and there are balloons flying overhead, pilots all festooned with furs wave their hands often. Yet old Tolstoy is convinced that man lives for his soul, not the world. Our doors open outward, L. A. Goodman has Tolstoy Junior say, but in doing so they open only on abysses, whirlpools; our doors ought to open inward, but they are obstructed. Now he's supposed to become smaller, so L. A. Goodman has all the other actors stand on boards, to overtop him. Also he is aged and dreaming now his old man's dream: that the world, based on his preaching, should keep past time alive. Tolstoy Junior portrays this aging by sticking a long forked beard on and wearing a different wig. The hair on the wig he now wears is illumined, quite white. The "friends" who surround him, the "Tolstoyans," are feeble wretches, their clothes designedly unkempt and threadbare, people who live off sheep's milk and are portrayed inexpensively by immigrants from Eastern Europe. Some of them have snipped little cards from sheets of white cardboard; these they stick in their pockets and secretly they note on them every word uttered by the old Tolstoy, who all at once wants to work as a peasant. His wife allows him to go plowing and mowing, but forbids him to drive the dung cart. At the hay harvest papirossy-smoking Tolstoyans stand around him in a circle and reproach him for living

with her still, instead of running away from her as
prescribed by the Gospel. At this point, the old Tolstoy has to fling down in despair the scythe he has
just been swinging wrathfully at his "disciples,"
sink to his knees, and burst into tears, but the scene—
in flinging the scythe down he injures one of the
"Tolstoyans" and there's blood spurting out of him—
has after all to be scratched.

It is the period in which the old Tolstoy rejects
everything, even spiritually so—the will to live,
writing, art. Sometimes, too, he loses all sense of
space. When Tolstoy Junior is asked to explain this
affliction, he tells—acting it out in the soft light
spread by the sheets over a quickly laid-out village
street—how the thoughts in his father's much larger,
but quite natural head, raced at twice the usual
speed, and he'd be running back and forth three or
four times between mansion and village market-
place, forgetting who and where he is. And naturally he's afraid he might go mad, and so, in order
to catch himself, he starts a conversation in the
market with a door-to-door salesman, takes the latter's pots and pans into his hands, and, in doing so,
slowly becomes aware that he was running around
in the belief that *now he was actually doing something at last*. But at his time of life there's nothing
left to do, everything happens of its own accord,
except this hadn't occurred to him before. True, he
keeps opening a window and looking up the village
street, but fewer and fewer tourists arrive to gaze
upon him as if he were the rising sun. Tolstoy Junior
too has to poke his smaller head, as directed by
Goodman, out of the window, until, in view of the

unlikelihood of an American public ever understanding the scene, they decide to scratch it and pass to the next one.

Here the old Tolstoy has to fall ill, because L. A. Goodman, romantic at heart, wants to have a death scene. People stoop over his bed, inject morphine, and give him champagne to make the fever break at last. This illness is acted out by Tolstoy Junior, considerably aged by his wig, no longer in good health himself, and due to die a horrible death some years later in Lofgreen, Utah, made up as his father and without any morphine, in a circus wagon—he acts it out convincingly, although in his opinion his appearance and the words he has to speak correspond in no way to how the old Tolstoy really looked and what he really said. During the illness a priest attends him with the sacraments, meaning to save what's left in him, if only tiny amounts of it. This priest, a lion tamer gone to fat, sought out for the role because of his girth—the only available priest's robe was very large indeed—suffers from a rash on his hands and has to wear black gloves. He conceals himself with the sacraments in the family chapel, so as to be at the dying man's bedside at the crucial moment. Or, if he fails to do that, to appear astonishingly in the room after the old man has died and announce in a loud voice that the sinner, before he died, was speedily reconciled with God. The priest with his black hands keeps dashing out of the room and announcing that the old Tolstoy is saved, although Tolstoy Junior can still distinctly be seen breathing under his wig.

When the ten weeks have passed L. A. Goodman

is unwilling to renew his contract. Demand for the film by its promoters, the film in which "the great author L. N. Tolstoy is portrayed by his sole surviving son in person," is negligible and soon ceases altogether, because the promoters have hardly ever heard of L. N. Tolstoy and the public hasn't yet heard of him at all. But although L. A. Goodman leaves Tolstoy in the lurch, J. W. Katz keeps faith with him. After unsuccessful negotiations with Barnum and Bailey he manages to get him in the fall of 1925 an engagement with the American circus Orfeo. Here, until his death, he appears regularly in the southern and southwestern states of America, between the acrobats and the elephants. Under the eyes of his father, who gazes down upon him from countless posters in the circus tent, thus helping the spectators, who have never seen him, to see at once the resemblance, and introduced with exaggerated esteem by Mr. P. N. Fernandez, the ringmaster, clad in blue tails, as "the son of his father, who, by a miracle of nature, tonight comes to be his father," Tolstoy Junior—now almost sixty-seven years old, who lives with a one-armed Brazilian woman, and whose life has gone to ghastly ruin in the usual way—clad in his father's clothes and supported by a walking stick, with which he also walks during the day, lopes three times slowly around the ring in the manner of a clown. Then he sits down at a desk which is dragged in, amid loud hallos, by one of the world-famous Ricolini brothers; the desk is supposed to weigh tons, actually it's made of cardboard and light as a feather, and the program describes it as being "made exactly like the desk of L. N. Tolstoy, the world's greatest writer, and it even has the same drawers." Glued to the surface are writing materials, books and manuscripts made of papier-mâché. Here Tolstoy Junior, picked out by spotlights, to the sounds of the circus orchestra, under the goggling eyes of the spectators, who understand nothing and take advantage of his appearance to relax after the trapeze act and, spitting between their boots, get ready to enjoy the elephants, here in public he begins to write. My handwriting is bad because my fingers are freezing, Tolstoy Junior thinks, but in truth the shivering and the shudders come from within. If art could wish anything for itself at all, he thinks, or writes, inside the circus tent, she'd wish for a nobler public than the one she's now got. The manuscript, into which he writes this, is a gigantic one, because P. N. Fernandez has reckoned with the great, indeed unbridgeable distance between it and the bleachers; it looks, J. W. Katz says, "as if it had been made for the elephants." But that's the way it has to be, as if made for the elephants, Katz tells himself. After the two minutes during which, as it says in the program, Tolstoy Junior "looks exactly like his father and sits there and thinks and writes—and after the performance he'll answer questions and sign his autograph in his wagon," and while the public is wishing they'd get on with the show and bring on the elephants, he begins to speak, so that people may hear his voice. At a sign from the ringmaster a fanfare sounds, the lights are dimmed, and eyeing the darkness where, moodily and scattered, his public sits, Tolstoy Junior says in his father's voice with an unmistakably Russian accent: Ah, how beautiful that would be, how beautiful that would be.

The Night

In Peru, during my travels through the flatlands
of the interior—my own business had collapsed,
so I was traveling for an international construction
firm, gangsters the lot of them—a couple of indi-
viduals crossed my path from time to time, the
strangest people of any I encountered there. They
were two young men, Indios or half-castes, perhaps
brothers, the same age probably, traveling in the
same region as me but for other reasons. The clothes
they wore were of the usual country type: gloves of
goat leather, tight waistcoats and jackets, white
shirts, black trousers covering their shoes, and on
their heads the customary round hats. Time and
again the delicacy and fragility of their limbs astonished me. No doubt they regarded themselves

as theatrical performers, and between the inter-
mittent evening shows they'd play small artless tunes
on a short flute. Probably they were paid by an
agency, not lavishly, for sure, but once I saw them
counting silver coins that somebody had slipped
them, a theatrical agent, I think. One thing I'm certain about: For a time their itinerary ran parallel
to mine and sometimes crossed it, by purest chance,
of course. Evenings, wearied by my efforts to sell
things, I'd read about them on the walls of buildings, where they called themselves, or the big yellow posters did, "theater artists," but then I'd lose
sight of them again, as I pursued my endeavors to
sell expensive equipment in that impoverished
countryside. In one place or another, too, somebody
would ask me if I'd ever seen their act, but since so
many new impressions were crowding in on me, I
had to reflect for a while before saying: No, not yet.
Or else I'd book into the same hotel as them. There,
at noon, before the show, I'd see them buy and tear
apart and eat a single dark flat loaf of bread, baked
in wood ash, I'd see them drinking the same cloudy
liquid which was always set before them and which
I—probably with the same gesture every time—
would push far away from me. Strange to say, one
of the two young men, the slightly shorter one, would
sometimes cry during his meal, and then the taller
one would lay his hand on his arm or his head on
his shoulder and talk softly to him, to calm him
down a bit. Also when the smaller one wanted to
stand up, he seemed to find it hard to do so, sometimes he limped a bit, too. The taller one would

cautiously insert his hands into the other's armpits, pull him upright and hold him straight, or, as they walked along, he'd hold his hand, not an unusual thing among men in this part of the world. Sometimes, after crossing himself, he'd even kiss him, if not on the mouth, then certainly on the forehead or cheek. Then, if I looked up from my cup, I'd see them making their way through the dining room, sticky with heat even in the mornings, and through the ever-open door they'd vanish down the "street"—clay like everything else thereabouts.

Once in Solo—a bad place, I'd advise anyone to give it a wide berth—our paths crossed again. I'd only just arrived and had vowed to make a killing the next day and sell at least half a dozen of my bits of apparatus, in order to finance my onward journey. At least, on arrival I felt quite enterprising. Since the couple were billed to appear that evening in the former horseback-riding arena, which had been modified for their act and was grandly described on a poster as the "municipal theater" (*teatro municipale*), I decided to go along and pass the time that way—evenings can be long in that sort of town.

The show, to which only men came, started late, at midnight perhaps; but soon after sunset, a very lovely one it was, too, I could see the first spectators, singly or in groups, all lower-class people, walking to the "theater." I sat in the rocker on my balcony—I'd taken the best room, anticipating gains from the next day's negotiations—and I saw them quietly walking along the street below me. I wrote a few lines to my ex-wife, once more about the children, smoked a few state monopoly cigarettes, and then took off, at a slow pace, my wide-brimmed hat pulled well down. When I arrived, the arena was almost full, but in the middle of it, a stranger among strangers, I saw to my surprise a still empty seat. I was still standing at the entrance, I almost turned to leave, but something simply drew me to that seat.

The "auditorium" was roofed over at a height of thirty feet or more. Benches had been moved into the riding ring. The walls of bamboo at one end of it were hung with mirrors; perhaps this was where haute école dressage exercises took place, but a small stage had been set up there. The whole arena was illuminated by torches and candles and it was packed with men. We sat and smoked until midnight; also, of course, the customary bottle of cheap sugarbeet gin was being passed around.

Then, just as we were getting impatient, onto the little stage, where now and again a military band must have played for the prancing horses, my two men climbed, no makeup, no costumes, no different from the way they'd been in our hotels, and there was a round of applause. They didn't make their entrance from backstage—there was no backstage—but from the front, out of the crowd, out of our midst. Hands came out from all directions to touch and stroke them as they climbed up, as if people wanted to make sure, for one last time, that the two of them were still alive. Then they were standing in the center of the stage, side by side, with their legs apart, wearing the clothes already described, and as soon as the audience fell silent they made a little speech, each in turn or together, in the local dialect, which I didn't understand—with my business friends I speak mainly Spanish, occasionally English, which is easier for me—directly addressing the audience, thus me too, also either singly or in chorus they sang a few little songs, as if to draw things out a bit, with their hats either on or off, songs I already knew from their flute playing, and then, when the public grew restless again, simpleminded as it was—the price of seats had been very moderate—they began to take their clothes off. So they're acrobats, I thought, feeling almost disappointed. The taller and broader of the two—I don't think he was called anything, anyway no name was mentioned that evening—contented himself with removing his jacket, waistcoat, and white shirt, which he hung over a chair, with a fastidiousness that was greeted by bursts of applause. Then, with some pride, brandishing a whip that had been passed to him from the audience, he showed off his muscular torso, striding up and down on the stage, in preparation for his act. Under identical clothes his partner had a less muscular body, pale, a body that was covered, as I saw to my horror, at a particular moment—I was just taking a deep breath, as one needed to in this place—covered with welts and sores. He had to take off all his clothes and put them on a smallish stool. Each time he took a piece of clothing off the audience sighed or breathed an ah or oh, following his movements with great emotion, because, as he undressed, new wounds or scars were being revealed. Of course, I thought, for now I knew why the young man had cried or twisted his face in pain each time he moved. Now stripped, his hands covering his privates, he took up a position beside the other (who, if not his brother, looked very like him) and a silence fell in this horse barn—filled with smoke and sweating men—I ought never to have gone there that night, but now, being curious or comfortable, and because I'd suddenly landed in the middle of everything, I couldn't leave. All around us, as I noticed only now, the most beautiful of all nights, the Peruvian night, had spread, a night whose beauty, unlike that of nights in other parts of the world, always confines itself to the sky overhead. Here below, everything else had recoiled, the brightness, the radiance, the painted picture, except that a dog howled now and then across the stark countryside, now reposing, but not for long, or a few crickets chirped. Or a bat that had been clinging to one of the rafters of our "theater" dropped into our midst and we trampled it at once to death. Yet through these rafters, since parts of the roof were missing—carried off by the wind—when I looked up I saw a fraction of this night evolving around us. I saw a scrap of sky and many, many stars, of which one would fall toward us now and then, but without hitting us. Beneath the sky the countryside spread out from Solo in all directions, flat and I suppose interminable. The man beside me lit his last cigarette, another emptied a last glass or passed it across to me, but as usual I declined it. And then, after one last star had fallen, the performance began.

The Night

An apparatus that athletes probably call a "horse"
is lifted onto the stage by two mulattos and placed
in the center of it. The robust young man throws
the cigarette he's been smoking to the floor and
stamps it out. The delicate, battered, and naked one
takes from a velvet cushion magnanimously prof-
fered by one of the mulattos a leather strap, clamps
it between his teeth, lays himself down on the horse,
and lets the mulatto tie him to it with a few hemp
cords of different lengths. Thus he embraces it,
holding it tight. The mulattos jump back down into
our midst, we make room, we admit them. The robust young man, who I still can't help thinking is
the naked one's brother, strides toward the horse
and makes a few passes through the air with his
whip, which is probably made of crocodile skin and
in former times has often whizzed over the heads
of slaves in this region, he *cracks* the whip. Then,
so there'll be no mistake about it, he extends the
whip toward his audience—me, too—and utters a
few throaty sounds into our arena, sounds that we—
me, too—repeat, replying to him as in a dream.
Then, without any interruption, with a flick of his
wrist, the whiplash lands on the back, shoulders,
and buttocks of his brother, who is so positioned as
to receive them. A terrible sight, a hair-raising sight:
one brother whipping another, sentencing him, ex-
ecuting him. The last thing one ever wanted to see,
and we're seeing it: a fratricide. Even then we look
on still, this night, which I now have to get through,
and from which, because I'm sitting in the middle
of it, I can't now escape, even if I wanted to. The
tall one, if this goes on, he'll beat his brother to

death. And this crush—more people have come, the old stable is full to bursting—our excitement, our male smell, the naked man's screams, for despite the leather strap he's screaming. The airlessness worse and worse, the sky more and more beautiful. If only I'd stayed in the hotel. There I could now be tossing from one side to the other in the—admittedly bug-ridden—bed, I could look at the still unspotted wall of my room, or even shut my eyes, while here, stuck among all these people, I see this slaughter, this venting of bloodlust, this feast of battle . . . I can't endure this "spectacle" any more—but then, at a certain point, one of us, who must have been standing or sitting right behind me, suddenly bursts into a somber song and we can all join in. The tune is simple, even monotonous, we catch on to it easily, so that even I can be carried along by it, though I can't understand a word. It helps me to get over what I have to see, it carries me away from this stable.

On that night in Solo, a province of Peru, a town of no more than ten thousand souls, the young man who'd sat and cried at the table next to mine had been beaten half to death, perhaps killed, before our very eyes, even for our benefit (we'd *paid* for it), anyhow I never saw him again. At a particular moment, toward daybreak, he slid from his "horse," hung there for a while with bloody arms and legs sticking out, and then dropped to the floor with a thud I'll not forget. The two mulattos came back and laid him on a stretcher, climbed down from the stage with it, and carried it through the audi-

torium. We all stood up and saw the young man—
deliberately I won't say artist—being carried on his
stretcher, out at the big side doorway, now thrown
open, through which formerly the horses had
pounded, saw him being carried into the night and,
in the first light of dawn, up the path between two
cypress trees that seemed to have been placed there
for the occasion, and then away over the horizon.
Bit by bit now we came to ourselves. And we left
the stable, some of us silent and dreaming, others
making comparisons between the different achievements of the two young men, and we dispersed into
the town of Solo and out beyond. On my way through
the town, where the first windows and doors were
being opened and in the shops the first jugs of milk
were being bought, I tried to join in the conversations of the inhabitants, asking in the various lan-
guages I thought I could speak what was the significance of the spectacle (*el significado del
espectáculo*), but it was no use, nobody understood,
perhaps nobody had any intention of understanding
me.

I overslept and was late for my appointment in
the morning, although I'd had hopes of it. Breathless, hands sweating, I got there. People were con-
siderate, touched me on the shoulder, but took none
of my things, which were superfluous anyhow in
this region. When I'd put my price lists back in my
pocket, I asked my business colleagues where and
how they'd spent the night. Their answers disappointed me: In bed. And when I asked if they'd slept
well, they said: Yes. Then they ushered me out

through the door, not without firm handshakes. The two young men who'd booked into one of the cheapest rooms in my hotel must have left during the morning, I saw nothing more of them that day. When I asked which room they'd been in, I was shown it. The sheets were streaked with blood, but the room was empty. I walked about in it, looked at everything, and said: Oh well. People noticed my interest in the couple and beckoned me into the hotel office, placed me before a map of the country, and described to me the itinerary along which the couple would make occasional appearances, and which took them, as it was taking me, through the most arid, impoverished parts of the country below the Andes, endless regions overpopulated with beggarly, desperate people. A week went by, I'd already forgotten the couple again, then once more our paths crossed. In another town, possibly even more dilapidated, most houses deserted, I read their poster, but I didn't go to the abandoned tile factory billed as the place they'd be performing in. Instead, I went to bed. That was a mistake, too. The whole night through I had to listen to the sounds that came across the bamboo roofs: the crack of the whip, the screams of the victim, the singsong of the audience; the moment I shut my eyes I had to *see* the scene on the stage. So sleep was out of the question that night, though I burrowed my head into the pillows. In the morning I didn't see the couple together, only the tall one, the strong one, who was walking up and down in front of our hotel to catch a breath of fresh air. Now's your chance, I told myself, go and ask him what's behind it, but by the time I'd plucked up the courage and gone out onto the street, he'd disappeared. I never found out who he was traveling with. And I didn't want to ask anyone outside the hotel, a business friend, for instance, especially since my affairs were being slowly wound down at that time. I'm not the right person for this country, I haven't got a thick enough skin. Better avoid that couple, I told myself then for the first time, but it wasn't always possible. Often enough, when I'd only just arrived in another town or set up shop in a new area, I saw them, the same couple, though perhaps differently constituted, they'd be strolling in the streets of some small town, long deserted and ruinous, kept going only by force of habit—Locumba and Maldorado and Tayabamba—always with cigarettes between their teeth, always arm in arm, hand in hand. But by that time I'd got used to the nocturnal screams and the song, and, if we did appear in the same place, them as independent artists, me as an independent businessman, I must after all have been able to sleep. I don't know who the whipper's partners might have been. In Lima I was told that the partner—by way of diversion for the restive country people, difficult to govern as always—was often beaten to death or left behind in some place or other as a cripple, so he'd have to be replaced. Everything hinged on whether or not, at the right moment, among the country folk or even in the audience, a new partner would step forward and be pushed onto the stage.

Arno

S lowly the poet with the long beard approaches the apartment house he lives in now, Arno writes, then he lays his pencil down on his writing pad. He's not sitting at his desk by the window anymore, he prefers to be at the back of the room. It was different before: Then he used to sit on his writing chair on its rollers, at an office desk bought at the estate sale of a spice dealer, and while writing he'd look across the garden to Number 14, whereas now he sits on the simple kitchen chair, up against the wall, and that's where he writes. He writes: The poet in his long overcoat stands in his living room now and breathes a sigh of relief to be alone again. Then Arno lays down his pencil once more. On the wall facing him there's a picture of his deceased dog, Fritz, a drawing of a complicatedly reclining woman, an expired calendar, and a thermometer. Above these hangs a metal sign, a present from his mother, saying No Smoking or Kissing. With his writing pad on his knee, his chin in his hand, Arno would like to write some more, but nothing occurs to him. For that's how it is with his writing. Time and again he's tried to produce evidence of his existence by writing quietly at home, working with his imagination—imaginative activity—but now he has given up writing "from inside." Nowadays he describes pictures, specifically the pictures his mother cuts for him from illustrated magazines and pushes to him through the gap under the door. So you'll keep in practice, she calls through the door, until something comes from inside again. Arno collects the pictures from the floor and clamps them into his steel clip from Hong Kong and hangs them on a nail beside him. He's always writing something. When the poet stands in his room, he writes for example on his pad, but nothing else occurs to him. Because, between the individual words, I look out of the window too much, I get confused, he tells his mother. And by this he means Number 14, into which, after being discharged from the sanatorium, the old poet moved, intending to revise once more, quickly, his life work, even though it's no longer in demand. Yes, it's not in the window anymore, says Lieblich the bookseller, and smiles. So then Arno imagines how the poet, a subtenant, sits in his white shirt in his apartment room, just like he does, not at the window any more, but at the back of the room, having retreated there with his life work. His mother says: Look at him, he's the last poet in our neighborhood, if not in the world, gradually all the others have died. He ought to be wrapped in cotton wool or at least, like young trees, in sacking. His trade is extinct, that's what I just read again today, she says and taps the newspaper. So Arno sat down at once and began to write his obituary notice. The notice is now in the bottom drawer of his desk, together with his medication; he's even addressed the envelope. Now he's only waiting for the light to go out in the poet's apartment. Then Arno will telephone the manager, make sure the poet has died, walk to the nearest mailbox, and send his notice to the most important German newspaper, which will certainly print it. After all, he knows the poet well and has often been for walks with him. Now Herr Quasener—that's the poet's last name—only has to die, Arno tells his mother, and he looks at the clock. Then he takes his obituary out of the drawer and looks for parts he might be able to improve, but he can't find any.

When you want to become a writer and for the first time have a great poet across from you, what you feel is unreality, Arno says.

Herr Quasener, when you go for a walk with him, takes tiny steps and says little, actually nothing. If you ask him how he is, either he says "It was nothing," or else he says "Read the Chinese." So Arno doesn't quite understand him. In front of the pavilion in the park, Arno notices that Herr Quasener's right shoelace is loose and dragging along the ground. This is a chance to open a discussion, Arno thinks, but he doesn't dare to draw Herr Quasener's attention to the shoelace or to throw himself at his feet and tie it up.

Once, on the way to the post office, Arno saw him smile. He also said he was sorry he said so little, but nothing occurred to him. He takes his letters to the post office because that way they go more quickly, although unfortunately nobody replies to them. Then he gives the letters to Arno and lets him put them in the box; perhaps he thinks it gives Arno pleasure.

Arno knows that the question is how to approach him. It's difficult, because Herr Quasener is so sensitive. Any word Arno utters may be the wrong one and occasion an icy silence. Of course Arno could say lots of things, but he prefers to say nothing.

In his room the poet hangs his overcoat on the wall and shuts the door, so the thing he fears will stay outside, Arno writes on his pad.

He must have said something wrong on a walk beneath the tall old fir trees that are dying and have been marked by anarchists with white crosses, because after that walk, which Arno can't forget, Herr Quasener has become even more dismissive. Arno even wonders if he still wants to speak to him. This walk humiliated him as no other had done: at the time, he almost wished Herr Quasener was dead.

As soon as Arno came home from the walk he pushed his mother, who always wants to know what Herr Quasener has said, into the kitchen and settled down again to work on his obituary. The poet, now without an overcoat, looks around his room, he writes. He underlines the two most important words.

All the same, even after that *word*, he's joined Herr Quasener sometimes on his walk in the park, although Herr Quasener hasn't answered when he's asked if he may join him. Arno simply stood there outside the apartment house and went with him when he walked out the door. For a long time he hasn't known if Herr Quasener actually notices him. So, with grim determination—three fat men could have fitted into the gap between them—they walked into the park.

On the far side of the park, with the countryside ahead of them, Herr Quasener must have noticed him, because he asked: What's that smoke over there? Has the great fire started? Arno looked across the fields and said: It's potato plants burning.

Once—but it must have been an oversight—Herr Quasener even talked briefly about himself, briefly lamenting his existence. What affects him most is that he can't read anymore—the print in books gets smaller and smaller—and that nobody visits him. Certainly he lives in quite a remote place . . . Once, so it was said, a journalist came to see him, but he was out at the time. Whenever it's rumored there's to be a visitor, Herr Quasener prepares himself weeks ahead of time, but then nobody arrives after all. Because the people who'd still like to visit me are dead, and the others don't want to, Herr Quasener says. And if he wants to visit them . . . Once he wanted to visit the grave of a friend who'd been dead for two hundred years, but then it occurred to him that like most German poets he was buried in a foreign country, and it was too far away for him. Also he forgets everything nowadays. Three times in a single day he forgot his publisher's name, till he wrote it down, but then he forgets where he's put the slip of paper with the name on it. Sometimes I'd like to write still, too, but I can't think of the suitable words, Herr Quasener says.

You mean from inside? Arno asks.

What? Herr Quasener asks, his hearing isn't so good anymore.

Like me, Arno is about to say but he prefers not to say it.

Out walking, when Arno bumps into acquaintances, Herr Quasener simply walks on ahead, then Arno has to walk very fast to catch up with him. Ah, Arno always says, now I've caught up with you.

When I go for a walk with him, Arno tells his mother, he's never the person I expected, except in a changing sort of way, probably for changing reasons, too. He has a son who works for Siemens, she says, but in Peru. She's heard at the butcher's that his daughter, a substitute teacher, has already been divorced twice.

Comes the day when Arno, having taken a hold on himself, with great strength and resolve pulls from his coat pocket the pages with his obituary on them and during the entire walk carries them along like a dead cat picked up from the gutter. And in his excitement his sweat so permeates the pages that it's impossible for him to give them to Herr Quasener when they're back at his door, as he'd been planning to do, so he takes them home again with him.

So Arno doesn't know what Herr Quasener thinks of his virtually finished obituary or of his own person. After the wrong thing that Arno said in the park he's supposed to have declared: That boy is lost! All right, so I'm lost, Arno said to himself and defiantly he sat down and went on writing the obituary.

When his mother read the obituary one Sunday morning, it made her extremely sad, she didn't even want to finish reading it. Again and again Arno had to urge her on—Read it! Go on reading! I admit my obituary is hard, but believe me, it's the truth. While reading on, his mother raised her fist to her mouth in fright. And she doesn't know Herr Quasener well, either. Arno could have given her, while she was reading, much more of a fright. All the same she sometimes greets Herr Quasener over the fence, but Arno doesn't believe he recognizes her; who knows who he thinks she is. (Even though once, when Herr Quasener was looking weak-eyed for the flowering hawthorn in his garden, Arno went up to him with her and said: And this is my mother.) His mother feels sympathetic toward Herr Quasener because he's only got one lung and he's such a cultivated single gentleman. An old man, but dignified, she says.

Yet it would be no surprise if Herr Quasener didn't recognize her. Not only he is getting older (and blinder, deafer, more forgetful), she is too. For a long time she hasn't been able to stoop, now she can't even kneel anymore. If they both get even older, they won't recognize one another anymore, even in the same room. All the same, his obituary frightened her. What Arno wrote about poetry being impossible in our world—because of the coarsening of feeling, the wars, sickness, misunderstandings, et cetera—even made her cry. Yes, every word of his hurts, but, he swears, it's all true. We all know that we need good writing about as much as we need nails banged into our heads—that's what Arno wrote in his obituary, for instance, but Herr Quasener said just that to the neighbors when he moved in here with his far too many books. It had to do, of course, with Herr Quasener's own writings being superfluous; mostly they're about southern landscapes and the people who used to live in them, all dead now. And that for years he'd been not quite "all there" was something Herr Quasener actually told Arno, if Arno understood him right. Why shouldn't he put a statement like that in his obituary?

Yes, his mother says, you met him too late, he's only an afterglow of earlier times. If you'd known him earlier, you'd have had a different impression of him.

You mean I'd have written a different obituary?

Probably.

Well now, Arno thinks—in writing his obituary he has to stick to the truth, and the truth isn't pleasant. His writings are nonsense, Herr Quasener himself admits that. And then Arno thinks of Herr Lieblich, who has told him: The law of contemporaries requires that you, Arno, as you look across your garden, bear witness not to the triumph of literature, but to its decline.

Even then, his mother says, you needn't have portrayed this decline so directly, people might think you're heartless. But enough of this for now. What sort of a day is it?

Yes, his decline, Arno thinks. Then he shakes himself and writes: When the poet has closed the door of his room, he reaches for his chair. Arno can't get any further that day, the light in the building opposite irritates him. He can't help thinking of the person Herr Quasener must have been when his writings were still flowing from him, yet who can prove that such a person existed? The present Herr Quasener is the worst basis for any proof; all he does is distract attention from the earlier one.

Interest in literature, in the context of human development, has blown away, the poet murmurs to himself and he sits down, Arno writes with his old pencil. Any conversation with Lieblich, the bookseller, will confirm this, he thinks. Nobody here, including his mother or Fräulein Passarge, still buys literary works or thinks about them, everyone despises them or ignores them. Nobody will touch the few works that still happen to be written and printed, it's as if the paper were diseased. In the city library they're right at the back, on the floor, dust gathers on them. People who come to my library bump into them, but no, even they don't look at them anymore, says Fräulein Passarge, the librarian. All they do is poke into the heap with their walking sticks, perhaps open a cover, read a title, then forget it right away.

Even then, I'm going to be a writer, Arno thinks.

And—since for lack of ideas he can't write anymore "from inside" and has accommodated himself to describing pictures his mother pushes to him—suddenly he couldn't stand a moment longer the light in the poet's room at Number 14. Day and night over there the lamp is burning. Facing that radiance, how can he himself go on writing? Well then, at least you won't see the light anymore, you'll see Fritz, and he's dead, Arno told himself one day and he brought the chair from the kitchen and set it close to the wall and, naturally, he wanted to finish and publish his obituary as soon as possible, then he'd see what happened. Now if he goes for a walk and Herr Quasener is coming toward him from far off, he switches to the other side of the street. Or he steps into a doorway and lets him pass. Half-blind as he is, Herr Quasener can't recognize Arno.

Now the sun has vanished again over the hedge and gone into the birch tree. Arno sits on his kitchen chair and writes. The sun has vanished, the poet lights a candle, he writes. His mother has brought him a new fountain pen from the town, this is the pen he's holding. Then he writes, because nothing else occurs to him, his name, his address, and the names of the town and the country where he was born and is living. He watches the way the ink slowly dries. Eventually he writes: Now it's fall, my room is cold, the ink is drying slowly. And then: The whole world is cold and drying slowly, it needs warming up at the stove. This is what I say, Arno Kassabeck, 7430 Metzingen, Michaelisstrasse 17a, German Federal Republic. And he watches his statement drying with difficulty on the paper. Beside him on the wall his Chinese clip hangs with the pictures his mother has pushed into his room. The first picture shows an old man sitting in the sun and sweating. Arno takes his fountain pen and writes: Old man looks at the sun which was so kind to us last summer. Then he waits until the sentence has dried and crosses it out. That isn't what I meant, Arno thinks, and he tries again. The sun shines on the just and the unjust and melts them, Arno writes with his new fountain pen, but he crosses this out too. Old man in the sun, weeping, he writes, and he crosses it out. Fizzling out in old age, who doesn't long for distant places of ice and snow, he writes—alluding to last summer's heat wave, which, however, isn't in the picture. Then he twirls his fountain pen between his fingers, but nothing else occurs to him. The second picture shows an old woman in a snow cave, probably in Alaska. She holds an ice pick in her hand and wears a coat of fur. Arno writes: Help! Help! this old woman in Alaska calls and builds an ice palace to avoid dying of cold. Then, having studied the statement, he crosses it out and writes: Salmon fisherwoman practicing her grueling but useful trade. Just so that we'll have salmon on our table, this old woman in Alaska has to . . . No, I'd rather not write anymore today, he thinks and hangs the pictures back on the wall. Then he leans forward and looks across his desk and the garden at the poet's apartment house. Aha, the light isn't on! Arno stands up to see if the apartment is really unlit and if at least a small reading lamp might be on, but it isn't. Could Herr Quasener, in his room, the heart of darkness, as Herr Lieblich once said, have fallen asleep, but this time, which Arno has long seen coming, forever? Arno, who really didn't want to write anything more today, unscrews his pen and writes: The poet has hardly lit his candle when his head sinks to the table and he's dead. Good night, Herr Quasener! Then he pulls the beginning of his obituary from the drawer and skims through it once more, but he doesn't make any changes, because it's all true as it stands. He adds the last sentence, sticks everything into the envelope, then he calls his mother.

Mother, he calls, come quickly, perhaps something has happened.

His mother, who gasps a bit nowadays when she has to run fast, but whose eyes are stronger, positions herself in her hastily donned dressing gown beside her son and looks across the garden with him.

Dark, Arno says, or can you see anything?

Perhaps he went on a trip?

But I saw his light in the morning, Arno says. Should I call the manager?

Wait a bit, you're always so impatient, it's a habit you should change, his mother says, and she lays her veiny, calcified hand on Arno's already quite sparse hair.

Shoulder to shoulder from the brightness of his room, across the fragrant desk they look toward the poet's dark apartment in Number 14 and think they'd better wait a bit.

The Cramp

The last time I was in Canada, to visit a branch of mine that had marketing problems, with my wife along to assist me, though she really wanted to keep an eye on me, forcing me to wear the traveling hat I detested and keeping me away from alcohol, on the semideserted car ferry back to Vancouver with our chief clerk Little (previously Klein) and Mr. Fireman, the engineer, we're sitting by ourselves in the bar and talking about how cramped everything is in Germany, a thing we'd all like to forget about and which I, not knowing why, blame for my bad marriage and my drinking. (In Germany everything is so cramped and drives me to drink.) Anyway, here I am, gazing toward the bar and talking in long sentences about the crampedness, while my wife is plucking at my sleeve to get me out of the bar and up on deck, from which apparently whales can be seen. But I move my arm away from her and say: No whales.

And why not?

Because I'm quite comfortable here, I say, can't you see?—yet it's cramped here too and I'm afraid it'll be getting even more so. And I lean back in my corner and am just about to pull my whisky glass, which I've meanwhile emptied, the first in weeks, across the table toward me.

Must you? she whispers and points at the glass.

Yes, I shout, yes, yes.

And what about your promise?

There it is, I say, the ocean.

Once, Herr Little says, when I was still called Klein and living in Germany, I had a room in the house of a baker, I think that's what he was, right under the roof, a cramped room almost like a coffin, I experienced something like the crampedness you're talking about.

Really, I say and look past my wife to the bar, behind which the Canadian barman, bald and circumspect, is standing in front of his bottles—he winks at me if I'm not mistaken—but then my wife whispers in my ear again: Please don't, please don't.

Of course, says Herr Little who still has a tot of whisky in his glass and with his finger is stirring the ice that's still in it, and whom I intend to fire even before I fly home, of course I'd wondered already, before I had the experience, about the crampedness in that peculiar country and that strange house, which was high enough, but, to save space, had been built right up against the houses on either side. I'd already been in Saskatchewan, where there weren't any houses like that. All the rooms were rented to some person or another, you could hardly pass anyone on the stairs, they were so narrow, and at dawn in the cellar the baker, together with his assistants, all of whom lived in the house, used to bake his rolls. I don't know if houses in Germany today are as cramped as they were in the fifties, Mr. Little says, I haven't been there in a long time, but I suppose they are.

Herr Klein, I say and put my hand on his arm, I've got something to tell you.

Yes, he says and laughs in my face.

But it's serious.

Well, what is it?

Later, I say. And he nods and reaches for his glass and drinks it up in one gulp. That's the way, I think and again I feel how cramped the bar is on this ship. If only it doesn't get even more so as things develop. And I look at my wife beside me and say with my eyes: Now I've got to go to the bar, right now; but she shakes her head and tells me with her eyes not to go to the bar again.

That reminds me, Mr. Fireman says, of a curious case of suffocation—he also knows about the crampedness in Germany and he too is stirring his

glass. It's my wife at the back of it all, and I'm
thinking: When he's finished his drink, you'll walk
past her to the bar and order another round, whatever she says or does. And I think of our children,
whom we haven't seen for four weeks, and wonder
what they'll say when their father comes back from
Canada and is suddenly drinking again. And that
the coming liquidation of my firm, together with
that of my household which is bound to follow—
household and firm, it's all the same—have been
brought on by the crampedness in our country and
in our town, as well as in the minds in our country
and our town, even though I don't know how these
two things are connected. (I mean to find out and
hope to find the answer while I'm still on this ferry.)
And then Mr. Fireman, even before he's told us about
the case of suffocation he witnessed, has finished
his drink and I stand up, as if that was all I'd been
waiting for—and I was waiting for it—and say: For
the last round you invited me, I'll invite you for the
next. Would you like some more juice? I ask my
wife and look past her eyes to the vein throbbing
in her temple, but she shakes her head, and I take
the glasses and carry them—such orderliness is
trained into us—back to the bar. When I come back
with fresh glasses across the slightly unsteady floor—
the sea is beneath us—I see that my wife has stood
up and has stepped across to the porthole and is
looking out over the bay with its islands, some of
which have billboards on them and are for sale.
Yes, you ought to buy an island like that and settle
down on it and never leave, I'm thinking, spend the

rest of your days here in the open among the whales
and sea eagles, but probably you wouldn't be able
to survive in nature like that, you'd die of boredom
in a couple of weeks. And I say: Come and sit down,
Ingrid, but she doesn't, and I sit myself down. How
cramped everything is here! Anyway, we clink glasses
and I say: Dear Fireman, dear Little, the unpleasant
things I unfortunately have to tell you today, I'll
put them off. First let's drink to the wide open countries of this earth, with their endless possibilities,
though they too are shrinking. And we clink glasses
and sip our drinks, and I feel myself expanding inside and I can breathe freely again for the first time
in ages. But the clink of our glasses makes my wife
shudder and she stiffens, first the head, then shoulders, then her back. (At such moments she's like a
pillar, completely statuesque.)

Look, I say and point at her.

Then Herr Little says that after supper he always
left the house he's described to us and went for a
walk around the town, small as it was, and sometimes he left the light on in his room, as they do in
Saskatchewan, so that people can see from far away
that a house or a district is inhabited and under
human control. But when he came home the light
had always been switched off, and he couldn't figure this out.

It's not surprising you didn't like to go into the room
when it was dark, Mr. Fireman says. I don't like
going into rooms that are dark, either, not even
here.

124

The Cramp

And Herr Little says: The inscrutable insides of buildings at night, in the darkness, make me feel scared.

It's because lots of things happen when it's cramped and dark, Mr. Fireman says and he makes a preposterous effort crossing one leg over the other.

Yes, I say, dark and cramped, and I look out of our bar, which is getting smaller all the time, past my wife toward the sea. Let's have a drink, I say and I drink.

One evening, just when I'm going out, Mr. Little says, the baker stops me on the stairs and asks me to explain. Like this. And he shows us. Did I forget to turn the light out when I left the room, or did I intentionally not turn it out? And since the baker, a bloated but still agile man, with tiny eyes, is pressing right up against him when he asks the question and panting into his face, the much younger and more callow Klein naturally daren't admit that he leaves the light on intentionally, and he says: I forget, I forget. Then the baker says that this has got to stop, that he ought to be more thoughtful, and he makes the following suggestion: You, Klein, before you go for a walk, you tell me how long you'll be gone, so I can turn the light on again before you come back. Then there'll be light in your room and we'll save electricity too. And he pushes young Little past his stomach down the stairs, keeping his eyes on him as he goes out of the house and into the darkness. Right, so Mr. Little walks around the town with its little houses, some newly constructed,

and its little towers and little streets, and he wonders how people who aren't much smaller than people in Saskatchewan can eat and drink and repro-
duce and excrete and breathe in this crampedness.
And then he goes back to his room, where the light
is on again, and he goes to sleep, and on the next
day . . .

Frau Spiegel, why don't you join us, Mr. Fireman
suddenly calls to my wife.

But my wife shakes her head.

But there's plenty of room, Mr. Fireman says and
he places his hand on the seat beside me.

But she doesn't want to sit beside me.

It's because she wants to punish me, but she's only
punishing herself, I say. Just look at her shoulders
and back, how contorted they are, it must hurt her.
She's doing it because I'm letting myself have a
drink with you, although, I admit, I didn't want to
drink anymore. And I'd even given her my word, I
say and laugh.

Even then, surely she can take a seat, Herr Little
now says and he pats the place beside me. Here you
are, he calls across to my wife, here you are.

Let her be, that's the way she is, it's her distin-
guishing feature, I say. One moment she's sitting
beside you and joining in with everything, and the
next, simply because she catches a whiff of this, I
say and hold my glass in the air, she turns to stone
from head to foot. She doesn't know that a nip like
this does no harm, quite the reverse. Or do you

know it? I ask my stone wife, and I notice that I'm sweating all over, because it's so cramped in here. Look how I'm sweating, I say.

You're certainly looking red, Little says, but then it really is hot in here.

But there are drops of sweat on me, aren't there? I ask and draw an index finger across my forehead.

Yes, Little says, there really are drops of sweat.

I thought so, I say.

The people who live on these islands don't know one another at all, they only communicate by telephone, Mr. Fireman says and points outside. Everything people usually say to one another face to face they say here into the telephone. Then if they chance to meet and see the people they've been telephoning all the time, of course they're disappointed.

And her, Herr Little asks, pointing at my wife, why isn't she looking out?

She's already seen the bay on television, I say.

And why isn't she talking anymore?

Because she wants to annoy me and has no feelings, I say. Isn't that so, I say, you have no feelings? And because she probably isn't even listening to us. Even if I hadn't had a drink, she only hears what she wants to hear. Hi there! Can you hear us? I call across to my wife, but she doesn't answer me.

The suffocation, Mr. Fireman says in English, happened this way. You know my legs? And he stretches his legs, so I'll be reminded of them, out from where he's sitting toward the porthole, where my wife has positioned herself for this afternoon. Anyway, like Mr. Fireman himself, the legs are very thin and long and hard. And I forget about my wife and reach for my glass and say, because my two employees (still) think I'm a comic and expect something similar now and then: To our various body parts, long and short, and may they be as vigorous as ever, at home and elsewhere . . . And they grin and we clink glasses and take a sip, and I feel I'm expanding and spacious inside like a hangar. And I want my wife to go away from the porthole she's glued to as an everlasting reproach to me, cramping the bar for me too, and I stand up to fetch her, but then Mr. Fireman says: Let her be! And he tells how he too had lived for a year during the early fifties in Germany, which was then quite shriveled up from the lost war, but for the time being subdued and meek, and had worked as an assistant at a technical college near Frankfurt. But whereas Klein had talked about the crampedness of his house, Fireman talks about the crampedness inside the heads of his colleagues, with whom he shared the instructors' common room. This crampedness was terrible. And the room, in which eight people might sometimes be sitting, had such a low ceiling that Fireman couldn't stand upright in it without hitting his head. Either he had to sit down, or else, if all the chairs were occupied, he had to go to the window and poke his head out, and, so as not to hit it on the ceiling, look at the part of the town that faced the college.

The Cramp

I can imagine what you saw, I say and think of my little firm, crammed between the cemetery and the autobahn, and located in a landscape where you can't see anything. And I shout: Cramped, everything there is cramped! and I feel the cramp in my chest. And think: Any moment something's going to happen to you, any moment something inside you is going to burst, and I wait for it finally to burst, but then after all it doesn't burst, but I take another sip and expand myself and breathe more freely and look away from Fireman's legs toward my wife and realize she isn't there anymore, the place where she was standing is empty. And where has she gone, I'm wondering and I point to the place and exclaim: Look! and I'm meaning to stand up and look for her, but Fireman presses me down because he wants to go on talking.

One of my colleagues in the common room had a black beard and he often talked into it, Fireman says in English. He had a paper bag with coffee in it, which he locked inside his desk. Sometimes he brewed himself a cup when he was alone in the room, we smelled it when we came in. He wore the key to his desk around his neck.

Look, my wife's gone, the place where she was is empty, I suddenly exclaim and point to the port-hole.

And where's she gone? Herr Little asks.

I don't know but that's where she was, I say and point to where she was.

It must have been too cramped for her here.

Anyway, I must look for her, I exclaim and I stand up and see clearly the long way that lies ahead of me, but really it won't lead anywhere. Because I know that in despair about my having broken my word—I really hadn't wanted to drink anymore— she'll have done herself some harm or other, probably thrown herself into the sea. And so I put on my traveling hat and grab my stick and am about to stand up, but then the two Canadian giants put their hands on my shoulders and say that it doesn't matter, women are like that, they vanish now and again, but they always come back of their own accord, you only have to wait a while. Probably she'll have gone up on deck and she'll be walking around in the sun a bit. And actually through the porthole I can see the evening sun, though what it has to do with my wife's disappearance I can't think, given the state I'm in. Then Herr Little says that he used to walk around the town every evening, but always had to tell the baker when he'd be back, so that the baker could turn on the light in his room. The thought that all the time while he was walking around, someone, if not several people, would be waiting for him to return drove Klein quite crazy. In any case at every third step now he'd be looking at his watch to see if he was walking too fast or too slow and wouldn't come home too soon or too late. Over and over he told himself: Faster, walk faster. Or: Don't walk so fast, otherwise you'll get home before the baker has turned on the light and that'll make things awkward for everyone involved.

But isn't it strange that so suddenly my wife isn't there anymore, I exclaim and laugh a bit. And tell myself that I shouldn't have drunk anything while she was there, it had offended her. And I stand up and go to the porthole, where she'd just been standing, and I place my hand on the brass frame of it and feel how warm the brass still is from her hands. Then I look across the wide, slightly turbulent sea, through which millions of salmon are passing.

The suffocation in the common room happened in the following simple way, says Mr. Fireman, who in his time had experienced German crampedness in a different way. Now he's living with his second wife and three ill-mannered children in an enormous but only half-paid-for bungalow in the forest, and he's got no idea that he's going to be fired any moment. Although he knows my marketing problems better than anyone on earth, he thinks he can stay with me for ever, but he's wrong about that.

Mr. Fireman, I say.

Yes, he says.

Got to be realistic.

But that's what I am.

And why don't you drink up and we'll have another one? I ask.

My colleague at that time, Mr. Fireman says, was suffocated by the crampedness.

Mr. Fireman, I say, first drink, then talk.

He's depressed because his wife has disappeared, says Herr Little and points at me.

Now and again everyone needs a drop, I say.

Some, says Herr Little, need two.

Anyway, Mr. Fireman says, one day I come into the common room and find that colleague of mine, the one with the shut-in look on his face, for which he was famous, stretched out on the floor. That's all there was to it, he says.

And what does that mean? I ask.

Had he been in the common room at night? Little asks.

He'd been locked in by mistake.

But he didn't need to die right away.

The way he was, he did.

What of?

Cramp, Mr. Fireman says, he suffocated. If you introduce a living creature, a man for instance, into such a cramped situation, after a while it starts to lose its bearings and writhe around, then it collapses. If you don't hurry up and enlarge its living space, the creature dies and nothing can bring it back to life. It's death by suffocation.

No, I can't stand it, I suddenly shout from my porthole to my employees. If for fourteen years Mr. Fireman has had a house he hasn't paid for, Herr Little has had since early summer a pain in the region of his appendix which no doctors can explain to him, but which you can see between his eyes. Sometimes, too, I ask him if he's in pain, but I really don't need to ask. I can see it. It's there, isn't it, I ask and point between his eyes, and Little nods and says: Yes, it's there. Can it be seen now? he asks me.

Yes, I say and I see it and we talk about something else. I think I shouldn't listen to any more of this, I say now, but go up on deck and look for my wife, who was standing here only a moment ago—I knock on the porthole—she can't simply vanish, can she?

The two of them look across at me and they don't want to let me go. What friends, I'm thinking. For that's what I always called them to myself, when my firm was still going better. Yet apart from the conviction that the world is too cramped, we haven't got much in common. They refuse even to think about my business situation. As for my wife's disappearance, they hadn't even noticed it, and if I draw their attention to it, the next moment they've forgotten it. What's more, my wife has never disappeared like this before, at least not on a ship. All right, I push off from my porthole, but I don't go up on deck, I go to the bar, where, since she's not looking anymore, I order another whisky. It goes quickly down my throat, then comes liberation, the expansion. Right, I think, now go look for her.

Once, Herr Little says diagonally across the room, after my walk, which as usual has taken me past the town movie theater and the girls who were always standing in front of it, giggling at me, briefly I come back to the house and then it occurs to me that I hadn't turned the light out. Thank God, because his eyes were so small the baker hadn't noticed the light. Anyway he isn't standing on the stairs waiting for me, so I can go up unimpeded and into my room and hang my coat on the door and sit down on a chair. But no sooner have I unlaced my shoes when without knocking he's standing there in my room holding a shotgun.

A shotgun, Fireman exclaims.

Yes, Little says, a shotgun. Of course in my cramped situation this shotgun looks supernaturally big and it's pointing at me. Good Landlord, I shout, don't do anything foolish now, I'll pay, if you want, for the electricity I wasted so thoughtlessly, I'll pay extra . . .

Now, I can't listen to any more of this, not now, I suddenly shout and pull the glass from my mouth and clamp my traveling hat on tighter and coil my scarf around my neck and walk with my stick to the door. And rush several steps at a time up to the deck where the wind blows at me through the curious superstructures that the ferry has. The waves are moving, too, beating against the body of the ferry, and the sky, without color till now, has become gray. With the islands for sale behind me, gloves on my fingers, I run along the deck. My wife, where's my wife? She's not on this side of the ship, nor on the other, not up at the bow, not at the stern. My collar up, I hurry through the spacious lounge, few people in it, and she's not in the lounge either. And there aren't any other places where she might be on this ferry, which is big, though you can see everywhere—most of the areas are off-limits for passengers anyhow. But since I don't want to leave anything unexplored I go back on deck again and speak to a few people, a bit confusedly, I confess. I click my heels, doff my traveling hat, make a small bow, and say: Excuse me, but have you seen my wife? And hold tight to the railing behind me, so I won't be unsteady on my feet. And because my wife is unfamiliar hereabouts and nobody knows what she looks like, I start—among these broad gigantic people standing in the mist, inner mist and outer mist, and retreating from me as soon as I speak— to describe my wife from memory. I begin with a few externals, then slowly work inward, describe her height and clothing, her hair and walk, imitate her walk for them, to their astonishment, as best I can, between the superstructures and the railing, enumerate her characteristics, her voice which would always break at the climax of our discussions, her morbid fragility, her silence, but nobody has seen my wife or heard her voice. What's more I've disappointed her, I'd promised her I wouldn't drink again and now look what I've done, I exclaim and I spread my arms and exhale my whisky breath across the deck into their faces. Some draw back or look at the ground, others shake their heads, others raise their eyebrows, while others again as a sign of great terror raise a hand to their mouths and gaze horrified over the railing. Then we all bow to one another and I slink away and feel that they're putting their heads together behind me. I can hear the word *fate*.

When I go down to my employees again—my wife isn't on the deck, nobody has seen her, nobody heard her—their bar has got even more cramped. The ceiling has sunk lower, I can hardly fit in. Mr. Fireman has put his chin on the table and, with heavy jaws, is still telling his story. Perhaps he made a pause in it, or he was waiting for me, anyway he's still at the point where he left off. Still the baker, gun in hand, is standing before him in the cramped room and he'll shoot his way to freedom any moment. Nonetheless, Fireman has noticed that what he's holding is a bird gun rather than a bear gun. And that he's not pointing it at him but at the light bulb hanging from the ceiling, which he shoots out, in order to free himself from the cramp. So it's dark. As for the shot, which is of course magnified a hundred times in the cramped room, as long as he lives he won't forget it.

Gentlemen, I say, I can't count on my wife anymore.

But where can she so suddenly . . .

There, I say, and point to the sea. Which, as I now recall, wasn't so visible because twilight had fallen. I think, I say, I ought to inform the children. I ought to call them up and tell them what has happened. This time she won't be coming back.

What do you mean, Fireman asks and he tips his glass upside down, though nothing trickles out of it, so where did she go?

Anyway you can't call anyone from here, there's no phone on the ferry, says Herr Little, and he sniggers. Also, wherever my wife might have gone, everything ought to go on as usual, I ought to be thinking of my firm.

Herr Little, I say, I know of your interest in my firm, but there's something I have to tell you. And you too, Mr. Fireman, I say, but then I don't tell them, because I don't want to spoil our peculiar evening, but a week later in two identical letters I tell them they're fired as of April 1. Klein has a pain between his eyes, Fireman is pulling his glass around, and me, my legs spread wide, I'm sitting between them.

That was in Canada, between fall and winter, on the ferry *Queen of the Isles*, four weeks after I'd given my word that I'd give up drinking. Yet because of the crampedness in the bar I had a drink, all the same. Then my wife disappeared. But instead of giving up the drink there and then, I pushed all thoughts of her aside and I drank more and more, to make the crampedness worse and worse. Later, after the siren had howled, when we arrived in Vancouver and had been the last to leave the bar and had gone up the cramped staircase and got into Herr Little's car that was waiting for us on C deck and had found my wife weeping in the back seat— the collar of her blouse was drenched—I flung myself into her arms. First I shook her for a long time, then I held her tight. That was on the day we flew back home, when we were meaning to make a fresh start.

A Conversation
About Balzac's Horse

1

L et's listen to what the papers say, exclaims
Honoré de Balzac on the evening of August
18, 1850, in the author's box at the Théâtre Historique, where at any moment the premiere of his
latest play is due to begin. And he pulls a paper
out of his coat pocket and he opens the paper and
turns, as best he can, thus laboriously, gasping and
groaning, to the guest on his left: a nimble little
red-haired man who is fitted into his suit like an
instrument into its case. Balzac, unhealthily cor-
pulent, perhaps bloated, though it's hard to tell in
this dim theater light, is literally bursting out of
his probably blue tails. So, whereas Balzac, because

of the many theater candles which are supposed to illuminate the world for him but which only make him hot, is sweating heavily, from his head, but probably under his arms and down his back too, is lodged deep in his chair, either for comfort or because he's in pain, the face of his unsweating guest (to change the subject entirely) seems to be slightly gnawed at, so to speak slightly nibbled on, by a skin rash. (He's perched on the front edge of a box attendant's stool.) Also his fingers, as much of them as peeps out from his sleeves, might be slightly nibbled on. But that's no surprise to us, for we're in a theater (one that's immense, too, and, alas, quite especially unsurveyable from the author's box). And now he (Balzac) reads, in bursts and abruptly, on the one hand because of his eyes, whose strength is rapidly failing as a result of his illness (so that he's justifiably afraid he'll no longer be able to see his public), on the other hand also because of his tongue, which is less and less capable of saying what he still might have had to say, something quite different comes out instead, sometimes the opposite, if anything . . . But we've already said it: We're in the theater! We have grease paint on our faces, wear theater coats, sit in theater seats, theater air envelops us. So we're ready for anything. Listen now, Balzac exclaims. If ever this gigantic brain, he reads, that's *me*, he says, with his gigantic imagination, *mine*, he says, this connoisseur of all human strengths, foibles, emotions, and so on, this thirst for knowledge, curiosity, and so on, this ability to fathom everything, and so on, should write a play, he reads . . . Then, Balzac reads, the censor will refuse permission for it to be performed. But on the next page, I think, he says, we find this: The censor won't *dare* to refuse permission . . . Or listen to this, he exclaims: And he reads how, all of a sudden, the public's attention has abandoned politics, the economic catastrophe, the mass murderer Lacenaire, and turned to the theater. The question being discussed now isn't the coming revolution, but who is acting in the play. Instead of demands for reform there are suddenly demands for affordable seats in the theater. All the banquets canceled, here, he exclaims. Here: All the balls canceled too. Here: Even foreign politics have been suspended in view of today's premiere of the prose tragedy *Les Bourgeois* by Honoré de Balzac, with Frédéric Lemaître as hero and Mademoiselle Dorval as heroine. Musical interludes and so on. Well, my dear Mr. . . .

Brissot, the dry red man says.

My dear Mr. Brissot, Balzac says. Please now, don't lean out too far over the parapet. And he makes a little joke too. You might, he says, fall into my public. My dear Mr. Brissot, he says, but I must congratulate you on your appointment as inspector of the cloacas of Paris. I've taken the liberty of inviting you to my box for this evening. From which we'll have a good view of the public as well as of the stage. Even if we don't lean . . .

Yes indeed, Mr. Balzac.

For officially, you see, Balzac says and he folds the paper up again, the box is empty. So is the stool on which Brissot is sitting, so is the chair in which he, Balzac . . . Because he's supposed to be in the country, where, behind drawn curtains—and the fruit that has fallen to the ground in the front garden of the house hasn't been picked up for a long time— he's alleged to be dying. His study, which he has recently rearranged, has suddenly become the room he dies in. A rumor, he says, which I myself . . . For reasons which, when you and I know one another better, will . . . As for the *bed* in which he's allegedly dying, Brissot must picture it as a wide mahogany bed with crossbars and hangings at the head and foot of it, as a sort of motor that enables the sick man, enables him to . . .

Move? Brissot asks.

To come to life, Balzac says. Who yesterday had himself bled one more time, and today . . . Well, today it's the other thing. But judge for yourself, my dear fellow, whether I . . . And, as best he can, he sits up in his chair, which therefore isn't vacant after all. And Brissot says: Not at all, not at all.

Anyway, Balzac says, the box has to be empty. In my condition, what with the prospect of a turmoil, the public becoming outraged, I'd better not . . .

Expose yourself? Brissot asks.

Expose myself, Balzac says. And that he considers his presence in the theater and *everything else* to be dependent on how his play will be received. If there's an almost certain triumph, then he'll display himself to the public; if not, he won't be there. So his box had to . . . unoccupied . . . Well then, Balzac asks, what state is my public in?

But Brissot can't see, because he mustn't lean over . . .

It's all right, Balzac says. Brissot may ease up to the parapet and then look down, as long as nobody . . .

Sees him? Brissot asks.

Meanwhile he himself, Balzac says, would stay in the background of the box and watch Brissot watching. A whole world is what he'd be seeing, a whole world! If at the end of the play people call for him, then they'll fling open wide the curtains of the box and he, Brissot, after he's pulled Balzac up from the truly abyssal depths of his chair, will quietly . . .

Hide in the corner?

. . . while I, who, as you already know, Balzac says, am in the country and . . . that other thing . . . to the general astonishment will suddenly rise from the background of my box in the Théâtre Historique and emerge, thus in the theater *after all* and suddenly standing at the parapet, perhaps also I'd be so moved as to blow my nose, dry my forehead and face, also my almost blind eyes, and under my waistcoat, as for my suspender buckles I'd . . .

Fish for them? Brissot asks.

All of it for show, Balzac says, and then, he says, just as everyone will have anticipated, I'll hitch my trousers up. From these and other signs of my being flustered, of my helplessness (he play-acts), Brissot, the public will see that I'm overwhelmed. But not before the enthusiasm has come to its climax . . . And then, he exclaims, since Brissot says nothing he still has something more to say, and since he has only one thought in his head, he exclaims: Success! Success!

Yes indeed, Mr. Balzac, Brissot says.

Or don't you believe it will happen?

Of course I do, Mr. Balzac.

Well then, take a look, Balzac exclaims. What can you see?

I can see . . .

What? What? When are you finally going to be so kind as to tell me what . . .

I'm looking toward the stage.

Good, that's right.

I'm looking toward the stage and . . .

Yes?

The curtain hasn't gone up yet.

Thanks. That's fine. And now?

I'm looking in the other direction.

Which one?

At the stalls.

Are they full?

They're still empty.

Don't worry, Balzac says, they'll soon be full.

So, Brissot asks, are you feeling excited?

Not at all.

But isn't there a lot at stake for you?

Everything.

And so you're not excited?

No, I'm not.

Because you're certain of the power of your art?

Balzac makes a dismissive gesture. Because, he says, everything has been planned to perfection.

And he tells how he decided four weeks ago to take charge himself of ticket sales, which, however, had been taken out of his hands, exactly as he'd thought it would be, not surprisingly, but as a matter of course. The most important thing was to attract the right public into the theater, this vast edifice, for him even almost unsurveyable, an old edifice, but always being expanded. For weeks he hadn't been able to work, because he'd been *busy composing his public*. The nobles! The critics! The ministers! Where to put the nobles, critics, and ministers, so as to avoid offending some by preferring others? Now listen, he exclaims. The dukes, the counts, also a bishop, all with their wives, he had put in the two front boxes artfully situated on a level above the front rows, with an excellent view, also where they could be seen. In the so-called Mistresses' Boxes further back he'd put the government and a few good friends of the theater director—they'd appear to scrutinize his play coolly and objectively and then, at a certain moment, as agreed, leap from their seats, as if against their own will, as if something were hoisting them up in the air, and they'd erupt with spontaneous applause. If they applauded, then so would the government, anyway it would look, in the theater, as if the government . . . And that would be the point, he says, at which the beefy men with large hands, standing at all the doors of the stalls, would start to clap frenetically, so that soon the entire theater . . . Can you see them now? he asks. Well, he says, they'll be arriving soon. Now, he says, you'll be wanting to ask who the men at the doors are. Well, he says, they're the famous *claqueurs*, of course, who have my orders and whom I've paid, if not overpaid, to wait for a signal from my box, and then to interrupt one of the stage actions with applause, perhaps not even justified applause. That signal, Brissot, will be given by *you*!

By me?

When I give a signal to you, of course. And he tells how, at the same moment, the bouquets he has ordered and which adorn the garments of the ladies in the first rows, will be plucked from their bosoms and flung on the stage. Half the critics were already in his hands, thanks to sumptuous dinners he'd been giving them for weeks past, the rest of them would . . .

And I thought, Brissot says, that it was only through your art . . .

My dear Brissot, Balzac says, probably you don't often go to the theater, do you?

This is the first time.

And so, naturally, you're impressed. Do you see the beautiful seats?

Yes indeed, Mr. Balzac.

And?

They really are beautiful.

And the chandeliers? You see the chandeliers?

Yes indeed.

And how do you find them?

They're beautiful too.

All Paris, my dear fellow, all Paris will be streaming into this place tonight, in order to discover itself, codified, of course, in my art. Are the stalls filling up?

Not yet, Mr. Balzac.

And in the orchestra pit?

There's a light on now.

You see, Balzac says.

And sitting in his theater chair he hopes it will at last begin and that the light Brissot sees is a good sign and that at last the musicians will arrive and at last take out their instruments and tune them at last, so things will get going at last, things will get going. For, he says, I'm exhausted. Weak, in pain, waiting . . . Anyway, he says, after listening in vain

146

for a while and waiting for the sound of instruments being tuned up, it's curious: Either the instruments aren't being tuned up this evening, or else it isn't only his eyes, it's his hearing too that's . . . But Brissot can hear as well, Brissot can! Why doesn't he hear the instruments tuning up? Can he perhaps hear things that are close but nothing that's far away? Can you hear anything? he asks.

Such as? Brissot asks.

Far off, Balzac asks, can you hear anything?

No.

Anyway, Balzac says—relieved because Brissot hasn't heard anything far away either—congratulations on your appointment as inspector of the cloacas of Paris. I hope it's a permanent position with a salary to match?

With a salary to match.

Paid to you regularly?

Paid to me regularly.

Fancy that, now, Balzac says and he sighs. And now, he says, you'll of course be wondering when Balzac will finally be . . . to the Academy, the Academy . . . After all this time shouldn't he be . . . to the Academy . . . Isn't it scandalous that he's still not been . . . How long are they going to be about it, won't it be too late soon? A thread, he says, on your coat . . . Or might it be a hair? Strangely enough, he says, bending over toward Brissot, and yet my eyesight is getting worse and worse, for really, and I'm not playacting, my dear fellow, I'm almost blind,

you realize? And of course, as you'll have noticed,
I wasn't reading from the newspaper, only pre-
tending to, yes, I was performing the part of a reader.
It's been ages since I could even recognize a newspaper, let alone read one, and the passages in question came, of course, from an earlier time, because
for ages now there hasn't been anything about me
in the newspapers, so that nowadays I simply recite,
Balzac exclaims, these earlier passages, which I've
known by heart for a long time, or else I simply
invent them. And my eyelids twitch badly too, just
look at me! You'll forgive me though, he says, for
simply reciting the old passages. And for . . . the
thread I suspect you've got on you . . . Or is he
perhaps mistaken and there isn't any thread? And
at the same time, after he's picked from Brissot's
coat the thread or hair or nothing at all and dropped
it over the parapet into the empty auditorium, isn't
it curious, he says, that just when he suddenly
couldn't *see* anything at all, or hardly anything, he'd
no longer been able to climb up any . . . couldn't
get up them, to the top, you know? So it wasn't only
his eyes, it was his heart, too! But also he could
hardly . . . on level ground anymore . . . Couldn't
catch his breath, his breath! But I do congratulate
you, he says, on your appointment. And now of
course, he says, you'll be asking: Why me precisely?
I mean: Why should you be sitting in my box, to
my left, in the Théâtre Historique? No, you needn't
move any closer, you're sitting close enough already. A miracle, you think, me, out of hundreds of
thousands of Parisians. And you're wondering if

there's been an oversight, your name might have
been mistaken for another one. For what am I doing
here, you're thinking. That's because the thoughts
of a man like me are foreign to you. Because my
thoughts . . . Because my thoughts . . . What was I
just . . . going to say?

You said, Brissot says: Because my thoughts . . .

Yes, now I remember. Because my thoughts, as things
stand, are always ahead of yours. My last work, he
says, hasn't been performed yet, and what do I have
in mind? The next work. It'll interest you to hear,
my dear Brissot, that it will be set in the cloacas of
Paris. "In the cloacas? Why?" "Yes, haven't you
heard yet what Balzac is doing?" "No, what is he
doing?" "Unheard of; never been there; unimagin-
able." "Yes, but what is he doing?" "It's unique,
incredible, a knockover." "Yes, but for heaven's sake,
come out with it, tell me again what Balzac is doing."
"He's bringing the cloacas of Paris onto the stage."
"Bringing *what* on to the stage?" "The cloacas!"
"The cloacas?" And then in my deep assuring voice,
me myself, I happened to be passing by and happened to overhear the conversation, and now, quite
unexpectedly, I enter through the plush-curtained
door, but walk with sure steps into the room and
into the conversation. I say: "Yes indeed, sir, you
heard aright! And even if it means the end of me,
I'm bringing the cloacas onto the stage!" "And why
are you bringing the cloacas onto the stage?" "Why?"
"Why!" And then, my dear Brissot, so that everybody will have a good view of me and hear me

clearly too, I walk, having hitched up my trousers, into the middle of the room and finally spread my charts out and explain: "Gentlemen! Don't you see? The strange darkness that spreads from the word *cloaca*, this *o* and *a*, gentlemen! Can you feel this darkness? (Of course they can't feel it.) Can you feel this darkness, Brissot?

Yes indeed, Mr. Balzac.

In view of this darkness, I say (of course I'm joking), there's only one thing for a man like me to do, and that is . . . the cloacas onto the stage.

Yes indeed.

So I decide . . . So I decide . . . It's not only that I forget my thoughts, Balzac says. I forget the words too. A word that occupies clearly and distinctly the middle of my mind today, next week or even tomorrow can . . . Good-bye forever, he says. So I have to speak the words that haven't disappeared yet. For example, I remember that yesterday evening at about this time, perhaps a little later, in a conversation, I've forgotten with whom, I'd been going to say *trumpet*, but then I say *problems*. Yes indeed, I'd been going to say *trumpet* and then I said *problems*. And why? Because the word *trumpet*, which a moment before had occupied the middle of my mind, suddenly it wasn't there anymore. Or else it was because—this could be it—I suddenly forgot that I'd been going to say *trumpet*. And last week, on Tuesday I think, no, Wednesday, I think, in a conversation about myself, I suddenly said *despised* when I'd meant to say *sought after*. No, I said *despised* and

meant *worshipped*. No, I didn't say *despised*, and I
didn't mean *despised* either. I haven't any idea now
what I'd been going to say. A word with three syllables, that much I recall, but not . . .

Despised.

No, not *despised*. I haven't any idea now what I said.

Perhaps *laughable*?

Laughable? In a conversation about myself? What
can you be thinking of?

Because you said: with three syllables.

But not *laughable*, that's impossible. A word with
three syllables, that's all right, but not . . .

Not *laughable*.

No, not *laughable*, and not . . .

Despised.

No, not *despised* either. I haven't any idea . . .

What you . . . ?

What last week . . .

You said?

No, Brissot, what I'd been going to say.

You said: So I decide, Brissot says.

So I decide, Balzac says, and tell myself: You'll
bring the cloacas of Paris onto the stage even if it
means the end of you. But then it occurs to me: Yes,
but do you know them? Those cloacas, out of myself,

out of my imagination I could doubtless . . . What's the word?

Evolve them?

What?

Evolve them!

All right. *Invent* them. Those cloacas, of course I could, out of myself, mind you . . .

Evolve them.

Yes, evolve them. On the other hand, one likes to lean on reality a bit. So I think about it. And I come, Balzac says, after lengthy considerations most troubling to me, no, these considerations torment me most horribly, to the conclusion: No, you don't know them! So you must study the cloacas, study the cloacas, I'm thinking. But who's to help me? In my thoughts I run through the thousands of people I know, some created by me, some created by nature. But which of them knows the cloacas? And after I've run through the thousands of partly natural, partly imaginary people in my partly natural, partly imaginary head, I come to the conclusion that not one of them knows the cloacas, not one! But then it occurs to me that there was this friendly little gentleman wearing leather trousers he always ties at the ankles with several tight thongs before he goes down in. And he has to go down in, or else he won't find anything out, this friendly little gentleman with boils in his armpits, this Mr. . . .

Brissot, Brissot says.

Right, Brissot. Or am I wrong about the boils, Brissot?

No, Mr. Balzac, Brissot says.

Whom you came across at night, I tell myself, Balzac says, not long ago, during one of your famous walks, just as he was coming up from an outlet behind the tannery, whereas you were just coming down from your desk, him exhausted, you exhausted. And I'm thinking: Brissot! Brissot will help you! He has the knowledge, you have the art.

Yes indeed, Mr. Balzac.

My dear Brissot, Balzac says this month of August in the theater out of the fathomless depths of his thoughts and of his chair toward where he supposes Brissot to be, how can one find out about the cloacas? I might not have much time left. I've . . .

For it is August in the theater too, as you'll remember. Yet the steps leading up to it aren't dry and dusty and warm, they're wet and shiny from the rain that's been pouring down on us for a long time. A real deluge. And anyone who's had the opportunity to climb up to the theater loft, like us, and to look around in the storage space and study the mildew deposited on the costumes by the damp air . . . You'll remember. The moment we enter the storage space where bits of scenery and costumes used in earlier plays are kept, the costumes to the right for the lighter plays, to the left for the serious ones—tailcoats and uniforms and sumptuous cloaks and long women's dresses—the constant danger is that

153

we'll get lost among them. Eventually we reach the area where the costumes aren't hung up but lie in great heaps on the floor. We breathed a sigh of relief, too, you'll remember, once we'd left this area behind. For years the stuff had been lying around. And we told ourselves (or thought): All of it, every single piece, had once had its significance. And we'd kept on picking this piece or that from the heap and we'd held it up to the light, held it to our nose. The moldy smell, the damp, even in the pieces that were most beautiful! And the puddles on the floor and the danger—we swore that the water from the puddles would soak through the theater ceiling into the auditorium, so that our theater, *from above* too, would be . . . How glad we were to be standing on the street again and to see in the arcades the shadows of people as they walked past, looking for shelter from the rain and the wind, who . . .

2

The best way to see the cloacas, Brissot says, is to go into them at the Saint-Martin canal and proceed in the direction of Montfaucon. Underground, of course.

Right! Balzac says.

But one can also enter them at Montfaucon and go in the direction of Saint-Martin.

That's fine, too, Balzac exclaims. Just a moment, he exclaims, you mean go on foot?

A Conversation About Balzac's Horse

On foot, yes!

Before I go there, Balzac asks, go as far as the lid, I mean up to the black hole at which we became acquainted, because of my condition, which isn't an act, although we're in the theater, couldn't I perhaps take a cab . . .

Of course, Brissot says, because of your condition you can take a cab, but if it has been raining it might happen that your horse would get stuck in the mud. Then you'd really be in difficulties.

Yes, Balzac exclaims, you're altogether correct, really in difficulties. To write, Brissot, he exclaims, always to be writing till one gets stuck in the mud. So you have to get out of the mud again, cross it out, cross it out! And then, as you can imagine, write again, write again. So that, when the moment comes, it can be crossed out again. The first act twenty-eight times. The second act thirty-nine times. The third and fourth acts fifty-one times each. But I don't give up. Whereas for the fifth act, if I remember rightly, it was no fewer than seventy-three times . . . Everything he crossed out, he says, was made a note of, everything, too, that he wrote afresh, so that there'd be no error in it, he kept accounts. A thick ledger was what Brissot should imagine, getting always thicker, and which shows unequivocally that the fifth act—he'd been counting, everything was noted down—no fewer than seventy-two times . . .

Seventy-three times, Brissot says.

Finally to be performed, Balzac exclaims, this evening, and listen now: in its original form, thus in
its first form. And now he tells Brissot, or rather
murmurs in his ear, having gestured to him to come
closer, while Brissot, hands on his knees, has a hard
time following him. That, apart from his own desire
to make his work as unassailable as possible, an
author had also to observe the wishes of the actors,
who had to observe the wishes of the theater director, who had to observe the wishes of the critics,
who had to observe the wishes of their readers, and
it was the public that didn't know what its wishes
were. So you change things, he exclaims, because
Mademoiselle Dorval, our esteemed tragedienne,
pictures her role otherwise, that is to say, it should
be more tragic. And when Monsieur Lemaître hears
of this, he exclaims, he too immediately pictures
his role as being longer and more tragic! And what
he'd like best is to have the stage entirely to himself
for five hours, and to be tragic all alone. So that I
rewrite the play, Balzac says, and wait for the op-
portune moment at which to slip it to the director.
And what does the director do? Naturally he rejects
the play that's been slipped to him, because it will
involve fresh expense—the more tragic it is, the
more expensive it is. So the writer withdraws again
to his room, so he changes things again, so he re-
writes everything again and tries to make it both
more tragic and less expensive. And while this is going
on, what had already been evident becomes more
and more so: that in a play like this one, a little
play like this one, anything goes, nothing is fixed,

anything can be said or not said, shown and not shown, that it can be shortened and lengthened, fleshed out or thinned down, exalted or humbled, without any of this making much of a difference. Because in a little work of art like this, in such a gem of a play, because of its inner mechanism, everything accidental and capricious comes at once to seem as if it were necessary and grounded. And a writer like this, too, could of course be shortened or lengthened, exalted or humbled at will. And the more clearly this was seen—that in any art necessity and caprice are actually one—the more changes came to be demanded. One actor will say: It would be ridiculous if Balzac couldn't remodel this minor part into a character part for me. So he blows some air into the part. And this actress, because of her beautiful shoulders, has the right to make a good exit. So what are we waiting for? We'll have a different exit. And Balzac? Isn't he hanging from every word? Isn't he killing himself for his art? No, he's not. And why isn't he killing himself? The answer is quite simple: Because he needs money. For it's his first duty as an artist to live in splendor, so as to excite his public's imagination constantly. But look at me now, my dear fellow, he exclaims and points down at himself, as if his lower extremities were especially to be deplored. As you said: really in difficulties. You said on foot?

On foot.

All right then, on foot, Balzac says. Listen, he says, for about eight weeks going upstairs has been . . .

But I've already said that. And then his hearing isn't so good, either, it's as if everything goes rustling past him. For instance this far-off sound that brushes over his hearing and which . . . an orchestra tuning up? And what do you think it is, Brissot?

But Brissot, who hearkens for a long time, says: I don't hear anything.

Whereupon Balzac is naturally relieved, for at root he hears nothing too, it's just that he was afraid all the time that he *ought* to be hearing something. Meanwhile his eyes, especially at night when he sits down at his desk and takes up his pen to round out in thought a character's destiny—then, he exclaims, suddenly this darkness, this darkness! So that sometimes he can hardly see the paper he's writing on. Strange, this darkness. Might he be going blind? Are you listening, Brissot? Am I going blind, perhaps? Listen, Brissot, I'm going blind, Balzac exclaims with a laugh.

Yes indeed, Mr. Balzac, Brissot says.

Right, Balzac says, so no eyes anymore. Right, no hearing either. Right, he says, no cab, either. But on foot, on foot! I can hardly see, but I'll take a quick last look at the cloacas. I can hardly hear, but still I'll put my ear quickly to the ground, to hear something far-off, rumbling perhaps, perhaps tinkling. And even if I can hardly walk anymore, I'll walk full speed to the canal and meet you . . .

Behind the soap factory.

When?

Tomorrow?

Yes, as soon as possible.

All right then, at midnight?

At midnight? Impossible. That's when I work. I can't think of anything else at present, but that's when I work. That's when I get up and put on my robe, light the six candles which, as you know, at the head of my manuscript, in my candlestick . . . No, you didn't know about it? And my candlestick, Balzac asks, haven't you ever heard about it?

No.

Strange. And about my pen? he asks—crestfallen. And after a while, bewildered: Not that, either! But ask, ask then, ask, he exclaims, while there's still time.

And what should I ask, Brissot asks.

What kind of pen it is, Balzac exclaims, with which I . . .

Write?

No, Balzac exclaims, don't ask.

And what kind of pen is it, with which you . . .

But didn't you hear, Balzac exclaims. Didn't I just say don't ask? Certainly I first said ask, but immediately afterward I said don't ask. And my robe, he asks after a pause, you probably won't have heard about that either, or? This robe, he tells, he'd had made for himself as a working robe, you realize. An allusion to a monk's robe, of course. What's more, it keeps me warm. At least, it has kept me warm till now. Now I'm cold. Even in the robe. Are you cold too?

No.

Not ever?

Very seldom.

And around my waist, Balzac says . . . Ah, he asks, what is it I wear around my waist? Around my waist, Balzac says when there's no answer, I wear a golden . . .

Scarf?

Chain!

Not a scarf?

Chain!

All right, chain, Brissot says.

Which cost me, Balzac says, two hundred and twenty francs, but it was worth, at most, only a hundred and eighty. I shouldn't have bought it, he exclaims. A rope's enough, a rope's enough!

Yes indeed, a rope's enough.

Yes, Balzac says, you can say that. You're not an artist, though. As an artist, of course, one has wishes, one knows other needs . . . And up comes the idea of something made of gold, a chain, you know, around one's belly . . . During those terribly long nights, when one is stuck in the mud. But actually you're quite correct, a rope ought to be enough. In any case, he says, I wear a robe. It complies with every move one makes. One's throat is free for breathing.

To breathe freely, you realize, to breathe freely. Till suddenly . . .

Yes?

Suddenly after breathing freely (in and out) for years, for decades, under the most varied conditions, taking it entirely for granted, suddenly breathing becomes really difficult (breathing in and out). Even in the robe, Brissot! I can't move in the robe anymore, either.

Not even in the robe? Brissot asks.

Not even in the robe! So I drape myself, it's midnight, all other human beings are plunged in the deepest sleep, beings like you, Brissot . . .

Yes indeed, Mr. Balzac.

. . . for after all you do belong to the same species as me, Balzac says. Of the same species as Balzac, Balzac says, even though it does sound strange. The same lineage, isn't that so, Brissot?

Well, Brissot says, if I may say so.

Louder, Balzac exclaims and holds his hand to his ear.

If I may say so.

In any case, Balzac says, I'll hurry to the canal and meet you . . .

Behind the soap factory.

When?

Tomorrow?

Yes, as soon as possible.

But not at midnight.

At midnight? Impossible. That's when I work. That's when I get up, put my robe on, light the six candles . . . And then, when the candles are lit and I'm draped in the robe and . . . Life, he says, is only endurable if you're *never in it*. So I am, as always, Balzac says, out of it. I stand outside and am in my robe and . . . Isn't the theater full yet? he exclaims. Brissot, he exclaims, take a look! No, Brissot, don't go to the parapet, go into the stalls, so that you won't be under any illusion. Go on the stage, walk to the curtain, *take hold of the curtain*, so you'll be quite sure whether it's down or not. But don't attract attention, take the delivery staircase. And you may take a look in the foyer too, and look out on the street, if you wish to, see if the public is finally on its way, finally . . .

I'll go, Brissot says and briskly stands up and looks around to find the best way out of the cramped space of the author's box, without winding around his neck, either, the scarf that's hanging over his seat and looks rather like a rope which has been much tugged at. And he tells himself that he'll still be in the theater even if he leaves the box. Even if you go down the stairs. Yes, even if he's on the stage, but he doesn't think that far. But when he reaches the curtain, he'll look, as instructed, through the little round hole, through which the actors ordinarily look into the auditorium, though he looks in the reverse direction, thus onto the stage, to see if anyone's there yet, even if, for the time being, it's only the stage manager, yet the latter too belongs to the theater, he belongs to the theater too. All right, so he goes from the box, backward, of course. All right, and then down the corridor, which is for the time being still empty, except for a few gray rats such as are found in any theater. Then the auditorium. The sets from the last play, they've simply been pushed in there for convenience—the superterrestrial gleam they have! (We don't know which play it was.) But, as we can imagine, the auditorium is quite empty. Also the stage space in front of the curtain, to which one mounts up a spiral stair on one side, is empty, whereas, seen through the hole in the curtain, the stage is both empty *and dark*. But the stage behind the curtain can't be quite empty, because a few sounds . . .

You see, Balzac exclaims, you see. The play is going to be . . .

A triumph?

You said at midnight?

Yes indeed.

And why not in the daytime?

Because of the cabs, Brissot says, who's now sitting in the box again, as if he'd never left it. The cabs, he says, rumble in the daytime over the pavement, making such a noise that in the cloacas one can't hear oneself . . .

Speak?

Yes.

They rumble?

Yes indeed.

That's probably typical for them, Balzac says, I'd like to make a note of it. And so I'll take, he says and actually does extract, really difficult as it is for him, a little notebook from his coat pocket, and he makes a note, despite his miserable eyes and his hands, which are shaking, of the words . . .

The cabs, Brissot dictates.

Quite right, Balzac says. Also the word . . .

Rumble.

Rumble. Quite right. These little peculiarities, which one only finds in reality, I make a note of them, so that now and again, in my work, they'll find a . . .

You study, Brissot asks, manners and customs? If I can use them, Balzac says and he puts his little notebook away. You said on foot?

On foot, Brissot says. We'll meet behind the soap factory on the Saint-Martin canal. Except that's where all roads come to a stop, in the mud you can't go any further. But you really do want to see the cloacas?

I do want to see the cloacas, Balzac exclaims.

And I'll put on, he says, my roughest coat, the strongest boots, and I'll go to the theater. And knock. (He knocks on the box wall, which is thinner than we think.) "Who's that?" "Gentlemen! A surprise! It's Balzac. I've written seventy-two novels with three thousand true-to-life invented characters. May I approach?" The theater: "No." I say: "But gentlemen, the triumphs I have behind me . . ." The theater: "No." So I change my tactics and say: "I'm Balzac and I don't know how the rumors about my triumphs arise, for I never had anything in my life but failures, nothing but scandals." At the word *scandal* the door is pulled open wide and I'm hugged. "My dear Balzac, so you've created scandals?" "Yes, but . . ." "Don't say a thing. If you've created scandals, you're our man," exclaims the director, Monsieur Harel, who has long experience to look back on and proved his mettle decades ago with shows involving erudite monkeys and tame elephants. "Yes, come and join us," exclaim the actors, in the most various dialects. "I hardly dared to count on you anymore," exclaims the cashier and rings his box-office bell. So I prop my turquoise-inlaid stick against the wall and extract from my linen coat a package of crumpled pages. A forest of intrigues and artificial destinies. In one word: a manuscript. "Here it is, take it," I exclaim. "Also astonishing deaths, seeming deaths, cleverly invented and cleverly connected with legacies, but even with the legacies it's often not a matter of legacies at all, but of the *illusory* legacies for which I'm rightly so famous, and very artfully contrived they are, too. A gold mine, Monsieur Harel," I exclaim, "a coup de théâtre." But the director exclaims: "What am I supposed to do with this stuff?" He gives me back the manuscript, and says: "Read it, Balzac read it aloud." Right then, Brissot, my dear good fellow, imagine a sumptuous room packed to the remotest corners with the best brains in Paris. Right then, Brissot, and me, I'm standing at the tenuous edge of a cloth-covered table, opposite the brains. "Sit down, sit down," they exclaim. "No," I say, "I have to stand when I read. I'm Balzac and as for reading this product of my tragic art from a soft seat in the corner of a sofa, I refuse to . . ." The most original brains start muttering. "But what sort of a person is this, wanting to stand up to read? From the sofa-corner is where till now everyone who's come here has . . . Can he be making fun of us?" "But no. It's just Balzac." "Is he always like that?" "Yes." "Then he's simply mad." "Probably." So then I read standing and soon I get heated and feel, out of my hair and down my collar, the pomade . . .

Dripping? Brissot asks.

And then, Balzac says, I've done my reading and roll up my manuscript again and tie it with string, after I searched in my pockets and my hat and even beneath the table and the chairs for the string and then with the string in my left hand, which is blotched with ink, moist, clenched to a fist, swollen, so look at it, look at it . . . Meanwhile Mademoiselle Dorval, who thinks she can't find a part for herself in the play, is tying her hat ribbons, smoothing her dress which is rumpled from long sitting, forgets to bid me good-bye and flits away. The director: "A masterpiece!" The actors: "What imagination!" The cashier: "What a success!" And then once more the director: "Except that in the first act . . ." And the actors: "Except that in the second . . ." And the cashier: "Except that the conclusion, the conclusion." You were saying? Balzac asks.

166

A Conversation About Balzac's Horse

I was listening, Brissot says.

Don't misunderstand me, Balzac says. Of course the play is a triumph which will earn me at least fifteen thousand francs, if not twenty thousand. Or, he asks, do you think it's not a triumph at all? Or don't you know? Can you see the *claqueurs* now? he asks.

No.

And the curtain, he asks.

It's still lowered.

Because of the rain, Balzac exclaims and rises up, gasping, and walks over to the already rather cracked rear wall of the box, in which a small window is set, barely visible, though he sees it, and through it he passes his ink-blotched hand out of the gigantic theater-building, groping into the twilit air of the street, and then he retracts the hand again, quite wet too. A real deluge, who'd have thought it, he exclaims and stamps his feet. As I say: Always something new, something that was never there before! All of a sudden, just when everything is arranged, the play written, the seats sold out, success assured has only to happen, then nature runs riot all of a sudden and turns against me. Everything turns against me all of a sudden, I see it exactly. This summer, weeks on end no rain, the planet expiring, those leaden afternoons, I can put up with it. But no sooner is the date fixed for the premiere when it starts to rain. And since then, would you believe it, it's been raining every day. Naturally nobody goes out now, let alone to the theater. But it won't

rain forever, or will it? What do you think? You
think it'll rain for ever? I ask you, Balzac exclaims,
whatever you may think. Let the world perish, if it
doesn't come to my play, let humanity drown! Well,
he says, perhaps I'm being a bit too harsh, but if
the public wanted to, it could travel in its galoshes
and put on its raincoats and hats and take its um-
brellas under its arms and then come to me in the
theater . . . Brissot! With a little goodwill, with a
little goodwill! That much I can ask of people, that
much I must ask of them, being an author. They
ought to go out into the rain, into the rain, he exclaims. This little bit of rain won't harm them, quite
the contrary. Watch out, he exclaims, in a quarter
of an hour everything will look different. It won't
be raining anymore. And even if it might be, the
theater will be full. Brissot, he exclaims, are you
listening? Perhaps it's only an assertion, but I assert
that in a quarter of an hour the theater will be full.

Yes indeed, Mr. Balzac.

You say yes indeed Mr. Balzac, but in reality you're
saying nothing. And you're thinking it serves him
right! Thinking it'll rain forever. Thinking it'll never
be full. And thinking—Why bring the cloacas really
on the stage? Brissot, he exclaims, *because it's something new and never was there before.* And in a situation like this, when the rain keeps on falling and
the theater is empty, because the public stays at
home and lets their tickets rot rather than taking
a trot through the rain, out of nature into my art
. . . In such a situation, Brissot, one has to try every-

thing. So go to the parapet, and . . . No, don't go. The enrichment of the artistic repertory, Brissot, is our highest principle. The expansion of art. The curtain rises, and what do we see? What's never been seen before. The curtain rises and an artificial cloaca, my dear fellow, runs to its full extent, in all its monstrousness, across the stage, but so artfully that nobody would be able to tell it from a natural one. Everything true to life, yet art. The artificial darkness entirely natural. The artificial swishing of the effluent—natural. The rats living in the cloacas will be assembled by technicians, working months on end, and they'll take the form of tiny but lifelike machines. Artificial skins naturally, artificial eyes. Teeth of metal, perhaps silver, no, gold, gold! Which will naturally glow brightly in the artificial darkness. Then at a signal from me the animals' teeth will have to clash. The famous gnawing, Brissot! Then at a signal from me the gnawing of the animals will be audible, artificially, you know? The feelings aroused in the public by the artificial gnawing in the artificial darkness—naturally deep and genuine and natural. What do you think? Balzac asks.

Yes indeed, Brissot says.

That's it, Balzac says. And even in the stalls, to deepen the feelings, a few artificial rats will be scattered around. Demonic, he exclaims, as you can imagine. In the boxes, he says, why not? Perhaps in the cloakrooms, too. But now our technicians have deserted our director, because he hasn't paid their wages. The technicians, Balzac exclaims, must be paid at once! I've always said that the technicians must be paid at once!

Yes indeed, Mr. Balzac, Brissot says.

Love, Balzac says, has been put on show. Power: power has been put on show. Ambition, politics, sickness, religion, money—listen: All of these things have been put on show. The public has seen it all, the public is bored. So the repertory must be expanded. So the cloacas must . . .

Yes indeed.

To portray the entanglement of human fates on a par with the entanglement of underground drains, to posit the one in the other, says Balzac a bit later—and he wraps himself in the folds of a story which he extracts from himself in honor of his opposite, namely Brissot. I'm thinking, Balzac tells—one might almost say he sings—of an old man, frail, stooped with sorrow. He might wear a sheepskin coat turned inside out. Before the curtain rises, this old man has been slandered and falsely accused of a conspiracy, and fleeing from his persecutors he has spent his life, because of this slander, in the cloacas. There he recognizes, by a birthmark, where? on the left shoulder, when? in the second act of course, a young girl as his daughter, Marie-Celeste, who was snatched from him twenty years before, and she, because of another mistaken identity, but the opposite way round, has also been living for years in the cloacas . . . And so on, he exclaims, and so on. "Father!" "My only child!" "Papa!" You understand, Brissot? Everything intense, but entertaining, everything true to life, but art. And how they come up to the surface again, how, dazzled by the light, they grope their way toward their old house, in the overgrown garden. Where, then, unexpectedly, an annual income of thirty-seven thousand francs, a legacy, and so on. All theater, except the feelings aroused in the public are genuine, everything is illusion only, but everything is understood, everything sympathetically felt. Out of the sudden dazzlement by the sunlight a good actor could extract a lot, or, to be more precise, he could put a lot into it. And the surprise with the money, which is also deeply moving, a lot can be put into that, or, to be more precise, a lot can be extracted from it. A play like that, for a thirty-three-percent share, I could quickly . . .

Except . . . Brissot says.

All right then, thirty. Everything depends on the entanglements, on the illusion which moves people, entertains them, for in art everything is possible, must be.

Except that . . .

You think it would be better if it was his only son he found again in the cloacas? But then Frédéric Lemaître would have to play the son.

Yes indeed.

Or the father.

171

Yes indeed.

From what I know of him, Balzac says, that arrogant dog will want to play both parts. The vanity of the man! These actors! A rotten crowd!

Yes indeed.

But he'd have to play one part or the other, Balzac says, or else I won't write the play.

Mr. Balzac, Brissot exclaims, Mr. Balzac.

And now, Balzac says, go to the parapet. Tell me what you see.

Mr. Balzac, Brissot says, ever since the cloacas have been renovated . . .

No, don't look. Let's listen!

What for?

The instruments might be tuning up, Balzac says . . . And shh! and quiet! and shh! That would be a good sign, it would mean the curtain was going up any moment. And he asks if Brissot can hear anything, but he, Brissot, can't he hear, he asks, after they've listened together for a while, anything either? Anyway he supposed he couldn't, because he, Balzac, wasn't . . .

Hearing anything?

Perceiving it. Which, on the one hand, was a pity, but which was, on the other hand . . .

Consoling?

Calming. For if one of us heard something while the other didn't . . .

A Conversation About Balzac's Horse

Mr. Balzac, Brissot exclaims, since the cloacas have been renovated . . .

Hearing, Balzac exclaims, the most subtle of all the senses.

The cloacas, Brissot exclaims, are empty.

Because modern cloacas, you see, he says, are almost clean subterranean rivers which flow regularly and cleanly through high-vaulted spacious tunnels that are brightly lit and handsomely paved.

But surely they still smell, Balzac says.

They've been altered, Brissot says.

In any case, Balzac says, in any case . . . You're getting me completely confused, he exclaims. What was I talking about?

The theater.

Of course, Balzac exclaims, the theater. And what, he asks after a pause, what was I saying about the theater?

They snatch your play . . .

. . . Out of my hands.

The rehearsals . . .

"And where," they ask me, Balzac says, "where may we send you news about rehearsals?" Yes, where indeed, he says. For he wouldn't divulge his address for anything in the world. Why? He had debts. Not that he kept quiet about them. And why didn't he keep quiet about them? Because a man like him

constantly had to be in difficulties and tirelessly
show his public that his existence was beset with
dire perils, among them his debts. Which, as he
knew of course, aroused greater interest than his
works. And were on a scale, like his imagination,
that could never be pictured sufficiently. Hounded
by dozens of creditors he slipped every night back
and forth between three or four rooms. Those stairs,
those steps! Realize: in my condition! Do you always find breathing easy, Brissot?

Yes indeed.

Your eyes?

Excellent.

You can hear?

Everything.

Then listen, Balzac says. We rehearse, I make corrections. Thousands of corrections. Whereupon, he
says, it suddenly turns out that the actors can't read
the corrections, because they can't read his writing.
What, unable to read the writing? Yet even the director who's been summoned can't read his writing,
the prompter can't, the cashier can't, and of course,
because of the weakening of his eyesight, he couldn't
read his writing himself, either. A black smudge
seemed to cover every sheet of paper he'd written
on. So he was writing a play and making corrections, but then everyone read something different
into his play, into his corrections, and everyone was
acting different things, as he thought he saw, or
heard, to his horror, during rehearsals, but he's not

174

certain of this, and he can't be, not only because he can't see anything anymore, but also because he probably can't . . .

Perceive anything?

Don't misunderstand me, Balzac exclaims, the play will be a triumph, it's just that I don't see anything or hear anything. I don't know, he says, what this all means. Do you know, Brissot?

No.

And what it might perhaps . . .

No.

And the tuning of the . . .

Instruments?

Listen, Balzac exclaims.

3

Listen to what the papers say, Brissot says and he pulls out a paper which he must have been keeping hidden all along in the inside pocket of his black, rather shiny, greasily shining coat. (You remember this pale, small red-haired man, these nibbled hands, the casing of the suit, this complacency, shabbiness, zeal, behind him the shoddy wall of the box, in August, during the deluge, on the front edge of his box attendant's stool? And can such a person really exist? He smiles, but we distinctly feel he's embarrassed. So the two of them aren't comfortable together, Balzac here, Brissot there. Who now, from

175

his pocket . . . You remember.) And he reads: "If, in one manner or another, somebody were to ask what course our civilization has taken during the last hundred years, here we simply point to the system of underground canals which, hidden from the naked eye, are a crowning achievement at once of architecture and of hygiene, underneath our cities . . . These canals carry everything away," he reads. Or here, he exclaims and reads: "In the presence of these vaults, which harmoniously et cetera, in the presence of the new age, which victoriously et cetera, in the presence of this progress et cetera . . ." Or here, and he reads: "So that every visitor who, after a comfortable stroll through these underground palaces, climbs to the surface again by the broad staircase, which might be called appetizing, his admiration . . ."

You have visitors? asks Balzac, who'd almost fallen asleep in his corner of the box.

Every night.

But who?

Oh, very refined people. For instance, Count de Gozlan.

You know him?

Very well. Or Count de Volney.

You know him too?

Him too. And then Brissot goes on to give, to Balzac's astonishment, a whole series of other names otherwise heard only in the very best connections, thus in the very best circles. For example, Lord Egerton.

Him too, Balzac exclaims.

Who sometimes brings, Brissot says, a little gift for my wife.

And what do these people want with you?

First they want only to look around, Brissot says. "Do show us," they said when they first came, "this new marvel, this subterranean machine that's been so much talked about in the papers recently, and which carries away all the *ordures*." "As you wish," I say and open the drain lid and go down first and lead them along the winding tunnels and exclaim: "Look! Here, Count, the vaulting is at its highest point, while over there it's at its lowest." Or I say: "And here, Baron, the streams come in, and over there they go out. This water before us is the great confluence of the streams." But then they start to yawn. "Is that all?" they ask. "Yes indeed," I say, "that's all." "But," they say, "we've heard of *something else*. There's supposed to be *something else* here." "Is that so?" I say, "Really?" "Yes," they say and they hand me inconspicuously a tip. So, Brissot says, eventually, though after some hesitation and with some doubt, I do show them the *other* thing.

The *other thing*, Balzac says.

So they won't have come for nothing, Brissot says. And ever since I showed them the other thing, they keep coming back. Thus at midnight, when they've eaten and sat long enough facing the long mirrors

177

in the cafés and have played their games in the gambling places and strolled on the boulevards, up and down all the time, all the time up and down . . .

. . . That's when I get up, Balzac exclaims, light my candles, put my robe on, and sit down at my desk. And then I sit at my desk, then I sit at my desk. But nothing occurs to me, nothing occurs . . .

That's when they suddenly don't know what to do, Brissot says, because they've done everything. And what to talk about, because they've said everything. And that's when they light cigars and come to me, down below. "But show us," they say, "this time not the technical achievements, we know those now, to tell the truth the technical achievements bore us. Show us," they say, "the other thing, right away, today we want to be entertained." Then I give each of them a glass of grog with pepper, to fortify them against what's coming, and then they drink it and lick their lips and say: "That's a delicacy for us, you know." And after that there's no . . .

After my play has been dragged around behind the scenes for three months on end, Balzac exclaims, there's no way back. What torture, Brissot. My coat, my waistcoat, these Cossack trousers, even these shoes here, everything hangs down off me, everything's too large. But there's no way back, no way back! Don't misunderstand me, the play will be a triumph of course, and it'll earn me twenty-five thousand francs . . . Recently, he says, I was trying to imagine a man, a man of my age. I needed him

178

in a quite definite context, for something I wanted to write. A man who's successful, you know. Right, then, I tell myself and I light my candles, wrap myself in my robe, let's imagine a man of my age who's successful. And who, I said as I was reaching for my pen, is fortunate. But suddenly I couldn't imagine him, a successful man of my age. A man, you know, who is fortunate, someone of my age. I sit there, in my robe, the candles, you know, the gold chain, you know, everything, you know, and, you know, I can't imagine anything at all.

I make every effort to give them good entertainment, Brissot exclaims.

Like me, Balzac exclaims.

I go to the limit, Brissot exclaims.

Like me, Balzac exclaims, like me! When something occurs to me, I go to the limit. I want to show everything then.

Like me.

I remember, Balzac says, the day of the premiere had been set when, since nothing else occurs to me, I think of a hat for Mademoiselle Dorval.

A hat?

A hat! At first, to be sure, I'd always said: An ostrich-feather hat. But then I have a better idea and tell myself: Not an ostrich-feather hat, no, a bird-of-paradise hat, like the one you saw in the Rue Souf-flot. And I go to the director and exclaim: A bird-of-paradise hat, Mr. Harel, I demand a bird of paradise hat for Mademoiselle Dorval, like the one

I saw in the Rue Soufflot . . . I demand that this hat be brought in out of reality . . . Every morning for two weeks I go to the director and request the hat. "If we have, on the stage, Mr. Harel," I say, "an actress as weighty as Mademoiselle Dorval wearing a bird-of-paradise hat as big as the one I've seen in the Rue Soufflot, then," I say, "then . . ."

Yes, Brissot says, one would like to show *everything*.

And then too I get the hat, Balzac says. After battling for two weeks I'm able to realize my idea and I get the hat. And now we have the hat, now we have the hat! You'll probably say now: A hat? What's the point of a hat? But you're making a mistake. A hat is . . . A hat is . . .

Yes, Brissot says, one would like to show everything that's not to be seen above ground.

Can you hear, Balzac says and places his hand on Brissot's arm. Can you hear the way I breathe? he asks, the way I want to breathe but can't? And can you see, he exclaims, the way I see nothing, can't see anything? Imagine: Everything outside is getting dimmer. But worse: Inside too, in my mind, everything's getting dimmer and . . .

First, Brissot says, I show them the knackery.

The what? Balzac exclaims.

The knackery.

You've got a knackery down there underground, your technicians . . . ?

A Conversation About Balzac's Horse

No, Brissot says, I show them the real knackery. There the gentlemen can watch the old horses and stray dogs, well . . . being knackered, forgive me. If they want, they can lend a hand. Take a hold, you know. I always say: "Gentlemen, you're actually in love with our knackery." And I say: "Come on now, come on, we have to be moving on, moving on!"

Where to? Balzac asks.

To the arena, Brissot says. But I only call it this because Count de Volney always says: "That's the place where you prove your mettle. That's your arena, my dear Brissot." But Lord Egerton prefers to call it my *stage*. And there, on this stage, in this arena, there's a spectacle for them to watch.

What spectacle?

It isn't prohibited.

What is it?

It can't be prohibited, because sometimes even the minister of the interior . . .

What is it?

. . . looks in, Brissot says. And Lord Egerton always says: "That's a grand spectacle you stage here." And Count de Berny says: "Actually it's a tragedy, dear friends, that's being staged for us here." And to me he says: "You know, Brissot, what you're staging here is actually a gripping tragedy?" And I say: "No, Your Lordships, I didn't know that, but I'll make a note of it."

You? Balzac exclaims, a tragedy?

And then he adds: "Do you know, Brissot, that in your way you're a real genius?" Forgive me, Brissot says, but that's what Count de Berny said. He probably meant that I stage things pretty well and have, so to speak, an artistic nature . . .

Count de Berny, Balzac exclaims and sits up a bit, came to a play of mine once.

He comes to mine almost every night.

At mine, Balzac says, he sits in the royal box.

At mine, Brissot says, he sits on the wall. Because at mine, he says, everybody sits on the wall. Because I don't make any exceptions.

Listen, Balzac says. Let's see if old Berny might already be . . . Pull me up. No, he says, I wouldn't see anything in any case, don't pull me up. But take a look for me. Is he in his box now?

No, Brissot says—though he hasn't looked, but on his little stool . . . —Don't be concerned though, he says. He's always late with me too. Like Guizot, the minister.

The minister Guizot?

He's always coming from a session.

He never, Balzac says, comes to me.

He's always quite out of breath. And he's hardly taken a seat, I've hardly given the signal, when he has to be leaving again. "Brissot," he says, "I've got to govern. Brissot," he says, "I've got to."

* * *

A Conversation About Balzac's Horse

Listen, Balzac says, something has been occurring to me. It has been occurring to me, he says, that people don't clap so much anymore, people don't clap so much anymore! And why don't they clap so much anymore? That's what has been occurring to me. I don't yet know what it means, I'm still trying to find out. Before, yes, people used to clap, and not only in the theater. I only had to go into a restaurant and at once people were clapping. In a restaurant, Brissot. In a restaurant! And when I'd eaten and drunk and was leaving the restaurant, there was clapping again, outside the restaurant. Whereas nowadays they don't even stop when they see me on the street, and in the restaurant they simply go on eating. As if they didn't know who I am, as if it was of no interest to them. Believe me, people don't clap so much anymore, people . . .

You must imagine, says Brissot—having now established himself on his box attendant's stool and made himself as comfortable as he can, his arms as well as his legs are crossed, he's leaning back—imagine our arena, imagine it best of all as a gigantic tub under Montfaucon. To the left of the soap factory, but under it, under it. It isn't paved there, it isn't illuminated, either. And to this tub, which in reality is a hollow, a hole in the earth, but *under the earth*, you know, and sand has been spread in the hole, and around it there's a wall, that's the place I take them to, carrying a ladder. (He stands up and pretends to be carrying a ladder, which is long and heavy, he keeps knocking against things with it.) And then, against the wall around the hole, he says when he's sat down again, against this wall around the tub I lean the ladder. And I call out: "Climb up," and clap my hands, "climb up!" And now the gentlemen are climbing up, though laboriously, I admit. And then, when they've arrived at the top (I've been climbing up behind them), I say: "And now, if you please, as well as you can, sit close together and make yourselves comfortable on the wall. I know," I say, "that I haven't got any soft seats for you to sink into, and no chandeliers to shine down on you, but instead, as you'll see any moment now, *something else!*" And I laugh. And then the gentlemen make themselves comfortable on the wall, just as best they can. And then gradually everything goes quiet.

It's the public's fault, Balzac exclaims, that people don't clap so much anymore. I've no doubt whatever about that. It's the stupidity of the public that's at fault, the poverty of its imagination. But that doesn't surprise me, that doesn't surprise me.

You ought to hear how quiet it is now, Brissot says. Quite quiet, quite quiet, quite quiet. As if the world was holding its breath. Quite quiet, quite quiet, quite quiet. It's because they can't see anything, you realize, because it's still dark. This quietness, Brissot says, this darkness.

But that doesn't surprise me, Balzac says. As an artist I'm not surprised by anything. As an artist I've learned to reckon with the stupidity of people.

With *changes in taste*. They always want something else, he says, always something novel.

And then, Brissot exclaims, I suddenly call out loud into the darkness. "Men," I call, "light the torches." "The what?" "The torches," I call, "the torches." And then, too, the torches are lit and suddenly the place is illuminated. And then the gentlemen can suddenly see where they suddenly are. Then they can suddenly see my stage. But the stage is still empty. I say: "Gentlemen, as you see, the stage is still empty. But," I say, "but . . ."

One can think, Balzac says, that one knows one's public, because one does know people, but then all at once one is having to deal with an opposite kind of public, which reacts in an opposite kind of way to the play one writes. If people wanted to react in the old way, with applause, you know, one would have to have written the opposite kind of play. But how would that look? And I drag myself to my desk and light my candles and prop my head on my hand . . . And I'm not thinking of my work, I'm thinking instead: What will my doctor say, when he sees I can hardly walk twenty paces now? And even when I'm sitting, suddenly for no reason I can't breathe anymore. And I light my candles and prop my head on my hand . . . And try to imagine something, but, listen now!—Nothing! Nothing!

And I, Brissot says, sit on the backs of my hands in the torchlight under the earth by Montfaucon on the edge of the wall and call out: "Gentlemen, are you sitting close together, are you sitting comfortably? Gentlemen, and now you'll be thinking my stage is empty, isn't that so? Perhaps you're even thinking: The world is empty. Well, empty it is, too. The delightful, round, replete world you've always imagined now turns out, with a certainty for all time unalterable, to be non-existent. The world, exactly like my stage, is empty to its uttermost limits, empty, gentlemen, empty. But not *completely* empty, I then say. In some places, such as, for example, my stage, as you'll soon see, it is so to speak filled with processes, and in those it presents itself. And then I call out to my men: "Now lift up the torches!" And I explain to my public what it's supposed to see, and that is what it sees. "Over by the wall there," I call, "a heap of bones." And it sees this heap. I say: "But not theater bones, as you probably think." I say: "Bleached out, admittedly, but *real, real!*" And then I direct their attention to the guttering around the wall, then to the blood, the traces of blood in it. And say: "And these, gentlemen, these real traces of blood, are left over from yesterday's spectacle." I say: "Dried. And over there," I say, "there by the grille, as if eternity was opening its mouth, one," I say, "of its many mouths, there, look, a set of teeth."

Listen, Balzac says. A bourgeois interior, with people and confusions to match, outside, inside, everywhere. After months, on the verge of exhaustion, no, beyond exhaustion, I entice, listen, Brissot, out of my poor brain, something you'll hardly believe, something you're about to see. And I invent two people, whom I bring, by means of feelings that can be felt by others, into artfully conceived apparent relationships, all by hints, very delicate.

And I, Brissot says, really do sit on the wall and call out: "And now the horse!" A cry of horror. "The what?" "The horse, gentlemen, the horse!" So then the horse is dragged in, a horse I've specially got ready for the performance. Naturally the horse guesses it's in for a bad time, naturally it doesn't want to be dragged in, at first. It bucks, tries to buck, and has to be kicked. And Count de Berny, pale with anticipation, exclaims: "Look, friends, see how it's trembling!" As soon as the horse is on stage, with torches to right and left of it, I admit at once: "Yes indeed, it's not much of a horse." And I walk up to the horse and apologize for the horse. And I stroke its bony flanks and thin neck. And say: "I know what you're thinking now. Yes indeed," I say, "you're right. Yes indeed, the legs are like sticks. Yes indeed, the eyes are dull. But what do you expect? It's flesh and blood. I mean: It's really here, before your very eyes. And there's still a spark of life in it, look. And another one, a livelier horse, simply couldn't be found in such a short time for the performance."

You bring, Balzac asks, a horse on the stage?

Yes indeed, Mr. Balzac, Brissot says.

A real horse?

A horse.

Sir, Balzac says and sits up, tries to sit up. My play has thirty characters and eighteen different stage sets and is set in four different countries, six cities, and on board ship. Every actor has six costumes and seven wigs, made of human hair. My play shows twenty-one different classes of society.

All actors, aren't they? Brissot asks.

In any case, Balzac says, it'll be a triumph. Because I got the best actors, the best stage designs, the best musicians . . . Can't you hear them yet? And naturally: A magnificent play, a magnificent play. You'll see: The public, if it comes . . . And just as you're thinking that the public really won't come, the door opens, no, Brissot, all the doors open, and my public, even though it's the last moment . . .

And I, Brissot says, I say: "A question! For what animal on earth since the time of the Deluge have the most traps been set? And what animal since the time of the Deluge has felt its best and has been most at home on earth? They're clever animals," I say, "but greedy."

The actor who plays the father, Balzac exclaims, is an excellent actor and he'll act the father's feelings excellently. Also the actress who plays the mother is an excellent actress and she'll act the mother's feelings excellently. Meanwhile, by the actress who plays the daughter the daughter's feelings will be . . . Has the curtain gone up at last? Are they on the stage at last? Excellent actors, all of them, but not punctual, not punctual! The actor who plays the father, whom I've known for thirty years, has never

been punctual. Sir, where have you got to this time?
Sir, we're beginning . . .

And then I suddenly stand up, Brissot exclaims, on
the wall, you know. And throw up my arms and
call out: "Let's begin!" And call out: "And now . . .
the rats!" "The what?" they exclaim. "The rats," I
call out, "the rats!" In a military tone of voice, you
know.

There, Balzac exclaims, listen, the music! Or am I
wrong again? Can't you hear, there, at last, the instruments being . . . The high notes, he exclaims in
the chair from which he's now going to be extracted
for all time, aren't those perhaps the high notes I'm
hearing?

And then, Brissot exclaims, the rats, my rats, shoot
out of their cavities hidden deep in the earth. And
then my rats smell my horse. Count de Volney, at
that moment, always says: "For me that's the loveliest moment of the whole performance, when his
rats smell his horse." But Lord Egerton contradicts
him: "No," he says, "the loveliest moment is when
his horse smells his rats."

Frédéric Lemaître is the best actor in the world,
Balzac exclaims as loudly as he can. Who can play
all the parts and show all the feelings and speak all
the dialects and, if necessary, also sing and walk
on his hands. He's the greatest, the greatest . . . And
when he comes on stage, if he comes on stage . . .

189

As we have ascertained, Brissot says, the thin rats are greedier than the fat ones. As we have ascertained, the thin rats are the greediest animals in the world. As we have ascertained, it's always the thin rats that leap on the horse first. To be accurate, they always leap first on the horse's ears, if that interests you, Mr. Balzac. Which, if perhaps you can ever make use of it in your art, are then immediately covered with rats. But soon the whole horse is covered with them, if you should want to make a note of this impression? "Look, it's wearing a coat," Count de Berny always exclaims then. And Lord Egerton says: "*C'est vrai*, a second horse is now coating the first one." At this point the horse always attempts to whinny, but, instead, it goes down on its knees. "Under the weight of its new coat," as I always say. "Look," I say. "But don't be afraid," I say, "because . . ."

Because we're in a theater, you remember, it's the month of August. And the sun would be going down now, if it had risen, but here we get along without any weather. Instead, sticky, heated air, the mark of the hothouse. Evidently there's no breeze blowing here, all the windows are tight shut. Also we notice the absence of plant life (plants, you remember). Instead, artifice. All the same it might be possible, let's be clear about this, that these exchanges aren't as entirely artificial as they should be in a theater, because the land of the living, after all, isn't far enough away from us . . . So that, toward the end, quite unexpectedly, quite against our will, in fact, a real wound . . .

A Conversation About Balzac's Horse

When the horse falls down, Brissot says, a few dozen rats are squashed. So then the horse is lying there . . .

. . . Then a quietness comes over everything, Balzac exclaims, a seriousness, a concentration.

Quite correct, Brissot says. Count de Gozlan is always quite pale with concentration. Count de Volney always grinds his teeth with concentration. Count de Berny always drools with concentration, saliva on his chin. And then something remarkable happens. Then Count de Gozlan, but also Count de Berny and Guizot, the minister, or the Bishop of Nancy, all of whom, as we know, have difficulties with their feelings and haven't, to some extent, had any feelings *for years*, all of them go pale. There's sweat on their brows and they call out: "Look, we're having feelings."

These actors, this rotten crowd, Balzac exclaims. Listen, Brissot, he says. You see, it's altogether possible that they'll leave me flat. Considering what I've invested in the play, that of course would mean . . .

The end of you?

Yes, it might also be that behind my back they've been advising the public: Don't go to the theater! Don't see the play! Better to go for a walk. Or are the stalls now . . .

No.

You see, Balzac says. And the . . .

Tuning

. . . Of the . . .

. . . instruments?

You see, Balzac says.

And then, Brissot says, my horse's skin, how do they say? It's . . . *slit!* The way a tailor slits his material from one end to the other. Rip, Mr. Balzac, my horse rips.

The spectators I've invited, Balzac says, the ladies with the bouquets, the director's friends, the critics stuffed with food! they're not coming, they're not coming! Not even the *claqueurs* are coming! Not many spectators, I feel it. Empty seats, especially at the back. To think how many seats are empty and how many spectators could have come, considering the enormous and still mounting population and the size of the . . .

Theater?

How few have come! My God, and the ones who have! Enemies, Brissot, all enemies! What if, at my most sensitive moments, they suddenly burst out laughing in their typical vulgar way? Admittedly, it's all mere invention, after all we're at the theater, it's all only a figment . . .

And now, Brissot later says, the anatomical dissection. My dear Mr. Balzac, the cadaver, for my public, with all the torches burning, listen to this, is dismembered. And the compositions of reality, their background, the monstrosities of which everything consists . . . My dear Mr. Balzac, and my public absorbs profoundly the backgrounds, and under thousands of tiny little teeth the *inner* horse becomes manifest to the astonished eye. The provisionally so-to-speak ultimate horse, as I've already said. But it's also correct to say *skeleton*.

A scandal, Balzac exclaims. What I need now is a scandal! Absolutely a scandal now. If the evening isn't a triumph, at least the evening ought to be a scandal . . . One that won't soon be forgotten. So do something, Brissot! Whistle! But loudly! Certainly you can whistle, Brissot, a scandal is what you . . .

Out of the places deep underground, Brissot says, thousands of rats stream into our new horse and utter sharp whistles which one doesn't hear at first. But which then produce a so-to-speak high and general tone over this region of the world, it . . . as Lord Egerton always says, it isn't human anymore.

A crisis, Balzac exclaims, a crisis! I've written a brilliant play, a triumph, a real triumph, but suddenly we're in the middle of a crisis, a profound crisis. Why? Our actors haven't come. What reasons can they have for not coming? Even worse: My public hasn't come, either, but the opposite. Isn't that a whistling? Brissot, go and see! No, Brissot, don't go. Isn't that a whistling, Brissot, even if we can't hear it? And it's right, it's right. Because, naturally, the opposite of my play is . . .

And now, Brissot says, the conversation takes a philosophical turn. "If you don't mind my saying so," Count de Berny says while putting a clove into his nose, "there's even something very human about it, the whistling of his rats." And Lord Egerton, with a cigar: "We differ, sir, evidently, in our conception of the human." "Which," the count again says, "to judge by my experience, cannot be established deeply, subterraneously enough." Philosophical, Brissot says, highly philosophical.

And this, Balzac says, is the crucial moment. Somebody has to address the public. Somebody has to explain the situation to the public. But who? The director? The way I know him to be, he'll have gone into hiding in his dressing room. Lemaître? He'll be drunk. The cashier? Fled. Now I see, Balzac says and sits up in his chair, I'll have to explain the situation to the public myself. Help me up, Brissot! Just come closer, closer, don't be shy, I know you can smell something. There, hold me under my armpits, take me to the parapet. No, wait a bit! What shall I see when I'm at the parapet? We've got to think about that. Well, he says, first I'll dry my forehead and face, my almost blind eyes too, then I'll fish for the buckles of my suspenders, hitch up my trousers, and give other signs of my . . .

A Conversation About Balzac's Horse

Helplessness?

. . . Which isn't an act, unfortunately. Truly, Brissot,
I'm scared, I'm scared of the public. But since it
can't be avoided . . . The best thing to say is: "Ladies
and gentlemen, *art*," that's the best thing to say,
no, he says, not art. I'll say *imagination*, yes, *imagination!* And here I'll make a slight pause, so the
word can sink in. "This evening," I'll say, "this evening my imagination will . . . Don't laugh!" Yes
indeed, I'll say: "Don't laugh," for if I say art they'll
certainly laugh. And if I say imagination they'll laugh
even louder. "Also I'll show you, with your permission, a large hat. . . ," that's what I'll say next,
"as I . . ." And then I'll describe the hat. But how
did the hat look? It was a paradise feather . . . No.
It was an imaginary bird . . . no. Well anyway, it
was a hat. Brissot, he says, help me. Brissot, he says,
my dear good man, listen, I can't think of anything
but the hat. What else should I say to them? My
artart, he says. My artartart. Finishfinish, he says.

And whereas you, Brissot says, have come to a finish
with your art, come to the finish of your finish, with
me everything's running smoothly. At a signal from
me, the skeleton is dragged away into a corner, by
my people, all wearing leather trousers tied at the
ankles, the same as me. Into the corner where, left
over from yesterday, the set of teeth, one of the
mouths of eternity . . . Then they resume their conversations, conversations. Nothing stimulates peo-

ple more than reality does. For instance, the question: What if one day, out of a not so very sequestered nether realm, something that could till now barely be kept underground, were to come to the surface in the cities? They're picturing it all to themselves. They're picturing the opera. The banks. The university. Or what people talk about in the banks, at the opera. "Let's get out of here." "Yes, let's get out of here." "But where's my money?" "Gobbled up." "So let's get out of here." "Yes, let's get out of here." "But where are the stairs?" "Gobbled up." "So we can't get out of here?" "So we can't get out of here?" But seriously . . .

For seriously we're at the theater, of course, and not in reality. Which, you'll recall, isn't our concern either. We're powdered and painted and waiting, not for any truth, but quite the opposite. What's missing is a conjuror, somebody in a starry robe, but who can also whistle and sing and walk on his hands. For seriously . . .

For seriously, Balzac says, I haven't been able to imagine reality for quite a long time. It cuts my breath off, it settles on my heart. My doctor always says: "Do breathing exercises, Balzac!" Breathing exercises! I tell myself: "Do imagining exercises, Balzac, imagining exercises!"

And while in the corner that we know about, inside the skeleton we've heard about, in the bone cavities that have been gnawed white, the hollows that everything consists of, the rats, Brissot says, which are now satiated (though their hunger will come

r it with equanimity, has hitherto been hid-
ut which now comes to light: as big as the
of a hand and still growing, glowing hot and
to the bone, an abscess which, in fullest flower,
, friends, we smell it, discharges a dull liquid
hines for us in the darkness. Balzac, crossing
hreshold of his box, he half drags himself, he's
dragged, out of the author's box, out of the
tre Historique, with a sound, no, a roaring in
ars, gaping mouth, his fat face crimson, no,
t, leaning into the hollow of Brissot's shoulder,
sot who light-footedly . . . Tell me, Balzac is
saying, tell me.

back), are making their nests, I suddenly leap up
and call out: "And now—the dogs!"

The what? Balzac exclaims.

"And now the dogs" is what I call out, Brissot says.

Well, isn't your play finished yet?

No, it's only just beginning.

My dear inspector of cloacas, Balzac says, you're a
great theater director.

Scorpio. Like you, Mr. Balzac.

What our modern public wants, Balzac says, you
with an unerring instinct have . . .

. . . hit on? Brissot asks.

What you show, Balzac says, is bestiality, of course.

Yes indeed, Mr. Balzac, Brissot says.

It is, Balzac says, the darkness.

That's how it may seem to you, Brissot says, in your
theater chair, in your condition. But in reality the
darkness is due to the fact that in your theater,
where a few spectators have now finally arrived,
though unfortunately not as many as you expected
. . . Only a few, ah, only a few have taken the trouble,
slipped into their galoshes, all the way through nature they've . . . And the darkness, Brissot says, is
due to the fact that the lights, just look, are being
turned out now, and the music, listen, though it's
only faint, only scant . . . And actually we do hear
music now, for, after all, though everybody knows
it, we're in . . . Yet only a small part of the orchestra
seems to be playing. So then let's imagine the sound

as being thin, a thread that will snap at any moment. And we see: Many of the small but finally illuminated music stands in the pit are empty and the unplayed instruments are standing around forlorn. And the person of whom we'll any moment be saying he was once Balzac asks: And how ought one to live in this darkness?

How ought one to? Brissot asks and he grins. And *shh*, he says. Your play's beginning. And he lays a few fingers of his nibbled hand on Balzac's knee. And the curtain you asked me about so many times and which, you'll recall, you once even told me to take hold of, look, it's really going up. And if I'm supposed to be telling you about your play, then I'll tell you about your play. Ah, he exclaims, what great art! That's my first impression. But ah, what artificiality! Allow, if you will, a simple man to speak frankly: Isn't artificiality unendurable? On your stage nobody suffers, they only act as if they were doing so. What is there for such a public to be absorbed in? No wonder people aren't watching, they're eating small sweet cookies instead. On the other hand, I admit that everything is just as you've described it. That's the bourgeois interior you told me about, and that's Mademoiselle Dorval, isn't it, with her hat, which really is big. Yes, the scenery was expensive, and your love tragedy, all illusion, all a figment you thought up, isn't it, yet you worked so hard at it . . .

Let's leave, Balzac says.

And your play? Brissot asks.

The wrong one.

And where shall we go? Br

Yes, where, Balzac says. W
asks, don't misunderstand r

And Balzac, still in his chai
of the overture in his ears—o
self again?—The theater of re
as he stretches out to him his s
hands, which you stage, he sa
which seems to have attracte
late—*just once*, but be sure yo
Balzac, who from now on spe
quietly, if at all, lifted out of
instead of avoiding, as advised
instead of hoping, in the count
saw machine of a bed, where th
him back to life, hoping that th
medicine will take effect, says:
arm around your shoulder and
says, lead me there, and when I
ladder, and the way I have to s
how, the wherefore, you know?
asks. So Balzac, on August 18,
swollen legs that have eluded us
for sure, and in his right leg, the ca
a wound inflicted on him, grotesq
sitting down at his desk, wrapped ir
will be trailing behind him now in
ridor, a wound, rankling, wild, w

out fc
den,
palm
deep
there
and
the t
half
Théa
his
viol
Bris
still

back), are making their nests, I suddenly leap up and call out: "And now—the dogs!"

The what? Balzac exclaims.

"And now the dogs" is what I call out, Brissot says.

Well, isn't your play finished yet?

No, it's only just beginning.

My dear inspector of cloacas, Balzac says, you're a great theater director.

Scorpio. Like you, Mr. Balzac.

What our modern public wants, Balzac says, you with an unerring instinct have . . .

. . . hit on? Brissot asks.

What you show, Balzac says, is bestiality, of course.

Yes indeed, Mr. Balzac, Brissot says.

It is, Balzac says, the darkness.

That's how it may seem to you, Brissot says, in your theater chair, in your condition. But in reality the darkness is due to the fact that in your theater, where a few spectators have now finally arrived, though unfortunately not as many as you expected . . . Only a few, ah, only a few have taken the trouble, slipped into their galoshes, all the way through nature they've . . . And the darkness, Brissot says, is due to the fact that the lights, just look, are being turned out now, and the music, listen, though it's only faint, only scant . . . And actually we do hear music now, for, after all, though everybody knows it, we're in . . . Yet only a small part of the orchestra seems to be playing. So then let's imagine the sound as being thin, a thread that will snap at any moment. And we see: Many of the small but finally illuminated music stands in the pit are empty and the unplayed instruments are standing around forlorn. And the person of whom we'll any moment be saying he was once Balzac asks: And how ought one to live in this darkness?

How ought one to? Brissot asks and he grins. And *shh*, he says. Your play's beginning. And he lays a few fingers of his nibbled hand on Balzac's knee. And the curtain you asked me about so many times and which, you'll recall, you once even told me to take hold of, look, it's really going up. And if I'm supposed to be telling you about your play, then I'll tell you about your play. Ah, he exclaims, what great art! That's my first impression. But ah, what artificiality! Allow, if you will, a simple man to speak frankly: Isn't artificiality unendurable? On your stage nobody suffers, they only act as if they were doing so. What is there for such a public to be absorbed in? No wonder people aren't watching, they're eating small sweet cookies instead. On the other hand, I admit that everything is just as you've described it. That's the bourgeois interior you told me about, and that's Mademoiselle Dorval, isn't it, with her hat, which really is big. Yes, the scenery was expensive, and your love tragedy, all illusion, all a figment you thought up, isn't it, yet you worked so hard at it . . .

Let's leave, Balzac says.

And your play? Brissot asks.

A Conversation About Balzac's Horse

The wrong one.

And where shall we go? Brissot asks.

Yes, where, Balzac says. Would it be possible, he asks, don't misunderstand me . . .

And Balzac, still in his chair till now—the sounds of the overture in his ears—or is he deceiving himself again?—The theater of reality, Brissot, he says, as he stretches out to him his swollen and ink-stained hands, which you stage, he says, in your cloaca, and which seems to have attracted large audiences of late—*just once*, but be sure you understand me. So Balzac, who from now on speaks only a little and quietly, if at all, lifted out of his chair by Brissot instead of avoiding, as advised, all excitement and instead of hoping, in the country, in his broad see-saw machine of a bed, where they're trying to bring him back to life, hoping that the bladder stimulant medicine will take effect, says: Now I must put my arm around your shoulder and then you must, he says, lead me there, and when I have to climb the ladder, and the way I have to see everything—the how, the wherefore, you know? Or won't you? he asks. So Balzac, on August 18, with monstrously swollen legs that have eluded us till now, lurching, for sure, and in his right leg, the calf or thereabouts, a wound inflicted on him, grotesquely, *when he was sitting down at his desk*, wrapped in bloody rags that will be trailing behind him now in the theater corridor, a wound, rankling, wild, which, let's reach

out for it with equanimity, has hitherto been hidden, but which now comes to light: as big as the
palm of a hand and still growing, glowing hot and
deep to the bone, an abscess which, in fullest flower,
there, friends, we smell it, discharges a dull liquid
and shines for us in the darkness. Balzac, crossing
the threshold of his box, he half drags himself, he's
half dragged, out of the author's box, out of the
Théâtre Historique, with a sound, no, a roaring in
his ears, gaping mouth, his fat face crimson, no,
violet, leaning into the hollow of Brissot's shoulder,
Brissot who light-footedly . . . Tell me, Balzac is
still saying, tell me.